OUR FOREVER PLACE

MAREN HILL

Always, always for John, Carolyn, Marlee, and Jayne

PROLOGUE

May 13, 1974, Vancouver, BC

Verity Child awoke alone in her apartment on Monday morning, feeling like a turtle without its shell. In some ways, she was homeless. Monday was the day people went back—to work, to school, to something.

But with her marriage dissolved, her dream job gone, and an unexpected windfall on its way, Verity knew she would have to find her balance again.

It was far too early to understand how a million dollars might change her life. All she knew was that she no longer had to work. A wild mix of emotions swirled through her as she tried to imagine where her new circumstances might lead.

Even though almost two weeks had passed since the traumatic events at the college where she worked, Verity was still reeling. Unveiling crime at Hillside College had depleted her. But, in the end, you could say she saved a life; whether that life was worth saving was another question.

Propping herself up on pillows, Verity decided to stay in bed awhile. After all, she had nowhere to go. She needed time to absorb the chaos of the past few days—and perhaps lose herself in the travel brochures piled on her bedside table.

She stepped out of bed, made a cup of coffee, poured it into her favourite teal green pottery mug, and padded back into her bedroom. Rearranging her pillows again, she pressed her back into their puffiness, took a sip of coffee, and savored the rich taste of dark cocoa and burnt sugar. She now had time to do that.

Verity thought about her misguided belief that everyone shared her values. She'd always assumed authority figures could be trusted and respected. That teachers genuinely cared about their students. That skills training programs were meant to prepare people for real jobs and real lives.

In the end, her relentless push to uphold those standards had helped expose problems and force change for the better—but at what cost to herself?

All she knew now was that she needed to get away. Far away from crime, office politics, and broken relationships.

She thought about how, when she lived with Charlie, she had struggled with a lingering sense of unworthiness. Not that it had seemed connected to him then—at least, she hadn't recognized it for what it was.

But things were different now. After helping to expose important truths at Hillside College, she carried a different kind of confidence. One that made her believe she no longer owed anything to anyone.

It's time to nourish my soul—hell, it's time to find it.

She raised her cup in a small toast to herself, because that was how she intended to move forward. She wouldn't rely on anyone else to build her sense of worth.

The main thing holding her back was Rick. They'd only just started dating, but the attraction between them was undeniable. She valued his calm strength amidst her own turbulence, the steady way he listened, the quiet consideration in everything he did.

But she had been fooled before.

Was it worth staying in Vancouver long enough to find out if he was truly right for her? How long did something like that even take?

The answer came quickly. She needed a change of scene. How else could she push away the memories she didn't want to carry anymore? How else could she begin to heal if she didn't put herself first?

She had to move on.

But where would she go?

CHAPTER 1

<u>June 11, 1974</u>

Leaving Vancouver behind, Verity had no idea what to expect. At 24, she hadn't traveled much beyond moving from Toronto to Vancouver with her former husband, Charlie. More than anything, she longed for freedom—no obligations, no schedules, no compromises.

The travel agent had made Exuma, a Bahamian island, sound like paradise. "White sand beaches all to yourself," he had promised. She doubted it, but the idea of a small, remote island with no skyscrapers and little infrastructure intrigued her. On Exuma, she told herself, she would simply exist.

Descending the steps of the Cessna 402, she stepped into the warm evening air, a stark contrast to the air-conditioned chill of the short flight from Fort Lauderdale.

She crossed the tarmac, stopping to retrieve her bags from the outdoor luggage cart. Two heavy suitcases tugged at her arms, and her leather shoulder bag pressed against her chest. As she stepped inside the small airport, the realization hit her: she knew no one here. No familiar faces, no warm greetings. A wave of loneliness threatened to dull her excitement. She kept her eyes on the attendants behind the counter ahead, waiting for her turn and avoiding what she felt were the penetrating stares of airport personnel scattered about the exit.

At the counter, she presented her passport. "A man named William was supposed to leave a car key for me," she explained. The car came with her cottage rental, and the caretaker had arranged for her to pick up the key here. The woman behind the counter flashed a dazzling smile. "How was your flight?" she asked, retrieving a white envelope from under the desk. Verity's name was printed in bold black letters on the front. *So far, so good.* Inside, she found the car key as promised.

Outside, Verity cautiously approached a small blue car, battered and dirty, parked next to the airport under a tree. In the dim light, Verity could see the name *Vauxhall* scripted on the trunk just below the keyhole. The car's large windows gave her a clear view of her surroundings, which was reassuring as she prepared to leave the airport.

She unlocked the trunk, heaved in her luggage, and then instinctively moved toward the left side—only to realize the driver's seat was on the right. A reminder that people drove on the left here. Settling in, she locked the doors, cracked the window just a bit, adjusted the mirrors, and familiarized herself with a few basic controls. Then, she double-checked the locks, ensuring all four buttons were pushed down.

Great Exuma was the largest of the 365 cays in the Exuma district, but still only thirty-seven miles long. She couldn't go too far wrong. If she crossed a small bridge, she'd know she'd reached Little Exuma and would have to turn back.

Following directions she had received by phone in Vancouver, she drove along the Queen's Highway, searching for the Darville Lumber Company sign. "Can't miss it," the caretaker had said. But the night was pitch black, and no sign appeared. Her chest tightened as uncertainty crept in. She had no phone, no lights to guide her, and no clue where she was.

The road grew rough, tires dipping into potholes. When she reached the bridge to Little Exuma, her heart sank. Peering into the darkness, with no other traffic in sight, she turned the Vauxhall around and slowly rolled back. *What have I missed?*

Relief washed over Verity as she re-entered Georgetown, a welcome contrast to the barren outskirts. Spotting a payphone outside a Scotiabank, she parked and fumbled for the caretaker's number.

By now, it was 10:00 p.m. William answered groggily. "Huh? Who is this?"

"Verity Child. I picked up the car, but I couldn't find Casuarina House. I drove to the bridge and had to turn around."

"Huh. Did you see the Darville Lumber sign?"

"No. I looked everywhere," Verity replied in a high pitch. "It's dark out."

"Ah." His gravelly voice sounded more alert. "Stay put. I'll be there in ten minutes, and you can follow me."

William's warm, easygoing manner reassured Verity, and she began to relax for the first time since she disembarked on the plane. *He didn't make me feel stupid for getting lost.* William arrived with a smile, saying it was no trouble at all. He led the way down the highway in a battered van, past stretches of darkened land. Still, no lumber sign.

Following William's van as it slowed near what Verity assumed was the cottage driveway, she noticed a solitary car parked just beside the entrance. Gripping the steering wheel tighter, she gazed at its unoccupied silhouette looming in the darkness. William pulled up close to the cottage, and Verity took the extra precaution of turning her Vauxhall around, facing the driveway. *Just in case I have to make a quick getaway.*

"Now I get it," William said, calling over his shoulder as he headed toward the cottage. "The Darville sign's been taken down. No wonder you missed it. Sorry about that."

"Good to know I'm not inept," she said, chuckling. Catching up to William, she asked, "Did you see that car by the entrance?"

William shrugged. "Not really. People leave cars all over here. Could be someone meeting up on the beach or a vacant property—picnicking, partying, swimming. It's common in Exuma."

The sound of waves crashing into shore reminded Verity that tomorrow would mark the real beginning of her vacation. Today was all about logistics and settling in.

William found the key above the door frame as promised and held the door open while she gathered her bags. "I left some basics for you—coffee, milk, bread, eggs, toilet paper. Anything else you need?"

"That's so thoughtful of you, William. No, I just can't wait to wake up with the Caribbean Sea in my backyard."

"Welcome to Exuma, Verity. I think you'll like it here. If anything comes up, you know how to reach me."

As he waved goodbye, she stood on the porch, listening to the waves rolling ashore. Tomorrow, her island adventure would truly begin. But tonight, her mind lingered on that vacant car by the driveway, and she couldn't quite shake the feeling that someone—or something—was watching.

Verity hurried back into the cottage, locking the door behind her. She flipped on the lights in both the living room and the bedroom, then unpacked a nightie and a few toiletries—just enough to help her settle in for the night. She'd have a better look around tomorrow. There was a sliding glass door in her bedroom, and she made sure it was locked before checking the rest of the windows and doors. The door leading out to the porch was secure, and all the windows were locked as well. The ceiling fan was a welcome comfort, and the small high window above the bed let in a slight breeze.

Pulling the blankets up to her chin, Verity felt a small sense of pride for getting this far. Her thoughts drifted to Rick and their goodbye kiss at the airport. Even though it was still early, there was a natural, easy connection between them that made their relationship feel effortless, like they had known each other forever. She remembered the sadness in his eyes when he saw her off, but he understood her need for space. The hardest part, he'd said, was not knowing when she'd be back.

Verity had chosen not to book a return flight, giving herself the freedom to stay as long as she needed. *I owe that to myself,* she thought, and she would decide if and when to reach out to Rick. No promises, no obligations. *I don't owe anyone anything. Except my parents, of course.*

She relaxed further into the bed, the soft warmth of the blankets pulling her into sleep as she anticipated waking up to a fresh start in the morning.

The shrill sound of laughter cut through the quiet, jerking Verity awake. She glanced at the clock on the bedside table. 1:30 a.m. *Better than being woken by a scream,* she thought, but it still made her pulse race. Rolling onto her side, she propped herself up on one elbow, her heart racing. *How close are they to the cottage?* she wondered.

She made her way through the dark house, flashlight in hand, and pulled back the sheer curtain covering the front door window. Holding her breath, she peered through the glass. The yard was pitch black, with no other lights in sight. *Just breathe,* she reminded herself.

Back in her bedroom, Verity unlocked the sliding glass door and opened it just a few inches. The screech of the door was sharp and grating. Pressing her ear to the screen, she could hear voices in the distance but couldn't make out their words. Remembering William's explanation of these kinds of gatherings, she told herself to stay calm. *I'll have to get used to it.*

Then, an ear-piercing scream shattered the night. Verity's pulse quickened. She couldn't ignore it any longer. She grabbed the phone-book from behind the rotary dial phone in the kitchen and quickly found the number for the local police. The officer who answered listened quietly before going silent for several seconds. Verity wasn't sure if the call had been disconnected.

"You don't need to worry about those people, Miss Child," the officer said at last. "They're harmless."

"But there was an abandoned car at the entrance to my driveway when I arrived tonight," she pressed. "This is private property, right?"

Another long silence. "Okay, if it'll make you feel better, I'll come take a look. Go back to bed and try not to worry. If I find anything suspicious, I'll let you know."

Verity didn't believe he would come, but she thanked him nonetheless, feeling only a little reassured.

Tucking herself back into bed, she pulled the covers up over her head this time, trying to block out the unsettling thoughts that kept her awake.

CHAPTER 2

Wednesday, June 12, 1974

Verity gazed at the soft light filtering through the thin white curtains covering the sliding glass door in her bedroom. She had slept soundly after her conversation with the police officer and now welcomed the morning light, her favourite time of day.

Her stomach fluttered with excitement as she imagined the view awaiting her beyond the sheer curtains. Still in her nightgown, she pushed the curtains fully open, unlocked the sliding glass door, and eased it open. Then, pressing against the stiff sliding screen, she opened it just enough to step outside.

Her bare feet touched the wooden floor of the verandah, and turning to her right, she saw that it stretched along the side of the cottage. She padded along to the back and discovered another sliding glass door leading into the second bedroom. She smiled upon seeing a clothesline extending along the verandah. It reminded her of her childhood when she would hang heavy, wet clothes and bedding on the line for her mother. They had been wrung out in the old-fashioned wringer washing machine, but the process left the fabric still quite heavy with water, unlike the spin-dry cycles of modern washers.

Walking back through the verandah toward the ocean view, she was pleased to see various teak tables and chairs strategically positioned to offer the best vistas. Eyeing the small round table in the northwest corner, she decided it would be the perfect spot for her morning coffee.

The gently sloping backyard was carpeted with long brown needles fallen from the branches above. Looking up, she admired the unfamiliar trees with their drooping, green needles swaying in the gentle breeze. No need for lawn mowing here, she mused. A path of flat white stones invited her to the beach, but she decided to slip inside and put on her flip-flops in case there were sharp objects along the way.

Verity felt a satisfying sense of freedom walking to the beach in her nightgown. The air was warm and still. She could see the sun rising like a banner of orange and yellow, heralding the start of a new day. No alarming noises came from the bushes, only the soothing sound of rhythmic waves kissing the sandy shore.

She felt like a child about to unwrap a birthday gift as she hurried toward the beach in her nightgown. As she stepped closer, removing her flip-flops, she was spellbound. The cool saltwater washed over her bare feet, sending a momentary chill up her spine. Feeling as though she had stepped into a postcard scene depicting stunningly blue water and sand the colour of pearls, she imagined she was in heaven on earth. She had seen pictures many times but knew that photographs could be altered to look more appealing than reality. Verity was certain that the breathtaking scene before her would remain in her memory forever. This was one of the few things she knew with certainty right now.

Verity noticed that someone had cleared branches and seagrass from the beach, making it easier to walk. *Probably, William,* she thought. Beyond her private stretch of beach, debris remained where it had been deposited by wind and sea. The water looked calm and inviting. Verity waded in a bit further. The initial chill eventually warmed, and she lifted the skirt of her nightgown to wade up to her knees. She was a solitary figure on the most beautiful beach in the world.

At that moment, she knew that all she had endured back home in Vancouver and everything it took to reach Casuarina House was worth every struggle, every heartache, every sacrifice. She wanted to stay on this beach, in this spot, forever. *Why go anywhere else?* Verity's blue eyes were wide and filled with pleasure as she surveyed the gift she had given herself as the sole heir to her beloved Aunt Lucy's fortune.

A flash of metallic green caught her eye. About two inches from her right knee, a long, slender sea creature swam by. She guessed it was a barracuda. Up close, she could see a mix of blue, green, and silver hues and a glassy eye. The fish made its brief appearance before disappearing from view, not alarming Verity. Perhaps it was a reminder that the ocean was home to many creatures unknown to her. She would take her time getting to know the waters and would be careful not to swim alone. She wanted to be independent, yes; foolish, no.

Satisfied with her initiation into this ocean paradise, Verity made her way back to shore and onto the white stone path leading toward Casuarina House. This was the first time she had a good look at the cottage's exterior. The brightly coloured paint looked fresh and cheerful—yellow, blue, and pink. *Perfect for a holiday retreat.* She noticed an outdoor shower to the left of the verandah and wondered if anyone would see her if she used it sometime. This was not an issue she had imagined pondering during her vacation, but she hoped there would be many more surprises ahead, just like this one.

Verity poured a few tablespoons of coffee into the drip basket and headed for the bathroom to prepare for her day. She loved not having to be anywhere at any particular time. She pulled on her red cotton shorts and white tee, feeling light as a feather on a summery day. After making the bed, she carried her cup of coffee and her camera out to the verandah, settling into the welcoming round table in the corner.

After fully enjoying her time on the porch, she boiled an egg and had it with toast. White bread wasn't her first choice, but she was grateful to have food on her first morning in a strange house in a strange land.

Oh, I must call Mom and Dad to let them know I arrived safely. It took Verity a while to figure out how to make the call using the correct country codes, city codes, and the number of zeros to place before the number one. They kept the conversation brief, ever-conscious of the cost of long-distance calls. "Please don't give my number to anyone," she implored, wanting to immerse herself fully in her holiday experience, unburdened by the past.

After confirming her safe arrival with her parents, Verity was eager to begin her first full day in Exuma. She made a grocery list, grabbed her sunglasses, keys, and purse, and drove her car toward Georgetown.

She parked in one of the four spots closest to the Exuma Markets grocery store and grabbed a cart left outside. Being at the grocery store felt so familiar, she couldn't help feeling more at home, even though she was over 5,000 km away from Vancouver.

Inside, the store reminded her of those found in smaller towns outside Vancouver, but she was surprised by the number of empty shelves and the few shoppers present. She hoped to buy fresh lettuce for salads but found no greens at all. The remaining potatoes looked half-rotted and bruised. She managed to find some tolerable acorn squash, wholewheat bread (not the seven-grain she preferred), a few apples and oranges, and many overripe bananas. Reluctantly, she added canned goods to her cart, something she had avoided for years.

At checkout, Verity inquired about the empty shelves. The

cashier, a Black woman, explained, "Oh, you're not from around here, then. So, you don't know that the supply boat comes in on Thursdays." She grinned. "Or, if not Thursday, then the next time it's safe to cross."

Verity paused, realizing that most supplies were transported by boat. The cashier continued, "It takes a while to reload the shelves, so your best bet is to shop on Friday, like everyone else." She laughed heartily.

Nodding, feeling very much the newcomer, Verity asked, "What time do you open on Fridays?"

"Nine," she smiled, "and it's best to come early."

Today was Wednesday, so Verity had shopped on perhaps the second-worst day of the week. She hoped her groceries would last until next Friday at 9 a.m. sharp, although she suspected that "sharp" wasn't a term commonly used on the island. She gained a new appreciation for William's thoughtfulness in bringing supplies for her first day at the cottage.

Next stop: the liquor store. Verity smiled to herself as she eyed the familiar label of her favourite Chardonnay. *That'll surely see me through the week, come what may*, she mused.

On her return trip, Verity observed the commercial strip. She later learned that the open area was where the straw market set up, sometimes selling garden produce. There was a marina with notices about trips to Stocking Island, a few shops selling tourist paraphernalia, and a café. A bit farther from the town center, she saw a pink hotel with "Peace and Plenty" written along the stucco wall.

As she rounded a curve, another café caught her eye, "George's Café." Attached was a pottery shop with a driftwood sign reading "Lacey J."

Glancing around the town, Verity realized she didn't miss the tall buildings and hustle of Vancouver. She was excited to explore on foot later, but for now, she decided to fill up the gas tank, as it was less than half full when she picked up the car at the airport. She went inside to pay by credit card.

"Thurz gonna be a hurricane today," said the Black woman behind the till matter-of-factly.

Taken aback, Verity's eyes widened, and she stood still. "What? A hurricane? I've never been in a hurricane before." She tried to appear calm, though alarmed. "What should I do? Do people go down to their basements?" She asked, knowing Casuarina House didn't have a basement.

The woman reassured her, "Oh, it's nothing to worry about. Hurricanes always go around the island. It won't be a direct hit. You don't need to do anything."

Uncertain, Verity decided to turn on the car radio during the drive home for more information. She couldn't believe that just days after arriving, a hurricane was expected. The car radio's static made it hard to get any updates, so she turned it off.

As Verity approached her candy-coloured cottage with far fewer grocery bags than intended, her eyes swept over the view. Somehow, the travel agent's description of the property hadn't mentioned that the backyard met the high tide line; the Atlantic Ocean was an extension of her backyard. This realization took a moment to sink in. The wind had picked up, causing the branches of the long-needled trees to sway above the carpet of needles scattered over the years.

Eager to explore the cottage and its surroundings, Verity carried two paper bags of groceries up the front steps. Upon opening the front door, a painting of two brilliantly coloured parrots perched on a tree branch caught her eye. Placed next to the indoor breakfast nook, it set the tone for what she hoped would be a vacation filled with colour and joy.

She quickly assembled a ham sandwich with mustard, hoping she would eventually find some fresh vegetables. Placing her sandwich and a glass of lemonade on a tray, she headed toward the verandah.

On her way, Verity paused to admire a striking seashell lamp positioned between the green sofa and its matching easy chair. Sitting beside it, she marveled at the assortment of seashells adorning the lamp's base. While she couldn't identify all the shells, she recognized some clam shells and a small conch. Her gaze lingered on a sea urchin shell, studying its intricate details from various angles. Captivated by the strategically placed starfish, she wondered if she would find any such treasures on Exuma's beaches.

Taking a bite of her sandwich, Verity glanced up at the swaying branches, contemplating what it would be like if a hurricane made a direct hit. Her knowledge of hurricanes was limited, knowing only that people boarded up windows and secured roofs. She doubted her backyard ocean was an ideal spot to weather a storm. She absent-mindedly wound a strand of her long hair around her right index finger.

After finishing her sandwich, Verity returned to the kitchen and turned on the radio, but there was no news. Her excitement to explore the seashore outweighed any lingering concern. If there were real cause for alarm, she figured, the news would be all over the airwaves.

Verity applied sunscreen in the bathroom, washed her hands, and put on a cream-coloured, broad-brimmed sunhat. Instead of flip-flops, she chose running shoes with a good grip in case she had to scramble over rocks.

The surroundings were tranquil, with no revelers in the bushes, and the sandy beach was deserted. She could hear the surf rolling in, stronger than the previous day, and the wind continued to pick up. Her sunglasses helped keep her hair out of her eyes, but her sunhat proved difficult to keep in place.

For no particular reason, Verity decided to head southeast on Tar Bay. She marveled at the various shades of blue around her: the deep sapphire sky, the turquoise ocean, and the darker patches where coral reefs lay beneath the surface. Squinting, she noticed a dark mass in the distance where white sea spray shot high into the sky upon impact. Observing that this formation acted as a barrier against the ocean's force, she wondered if such reefs could protect Tar Bay from a tsunami.

Continuing along the shore, she spotted numerous shells scattered across the sand as far back as the cement barriers built to protect properties from flooding. She recognized the shiny white shells resembling lightbulbs, similar to those she'd admired on the cottage's seashell lamp. There were also long, oval pink and yellow shells, some with both sides intact. Without pockets or containers, Verity chose to leave them for another day.

Navigating a large expanse of beach rock, she was grateful for her running shoes. She carefully avoided more treacherous areas, mindful not to trip.

She passed three cottages on her right, one completely boarded up. The other two showed signs of life: Adirondack chairs arranged in a circle, a bright orange inflatable seahorse poised to be swept away by the wind, a blue air mattress lying on the porch, bathing suits and towels flapping on a clothesline. Verity paused to inhale the fresh sea air, exhaling slowly, grateful to just *be*.

A sudden movement to the left caught Verity's attention as a massive splash of water pelleted onto the rocks just ahead of her, followed by another just as big, and then they tapered off. Verity noted that she needed to stay some distance away for fear of being caught in the sea spray. She reached the end of the rock mass and scampered down to the sandy shore once again.

The white sand was so enticing that Verity removed her shoes and walked barefoot along a stretch of sand as soft as flour. She watched as huge rolls of salt water from the turquoise blue sea transformed into white sea spray as they crashed into the sandy shore, creating ripples of creamy seafoam as the undertow pulled the wave back again into the sea. Some waves were pitched farther beyond the shore, releasing seashells and ocean debris high up onto the sand.

As she approached a little cove up ahead, Verity noticed a rounded, light purplish shell washed up on the sand. Hurrying over, she picked it up and beamed with pleasure to see that it was an empty sea urchin shell. Intact. *That probably never happens.* No spines, so she knew before picking it up that there wouldn't be a live creature inside. This one she would take with her today as it would not likely be there tomorrow, or even in the next short while, depending on the directives of the sea and the possibility of early morning shellers.

To her right was a field of long, dry grass intersected by a rudimentary roadway. Beyond that was the Queen's Highway. Not a car in sight. *Are people staying home, making preparations for the hurricane? Are they just waiting for the supply boat to arrive?* Those were two things Verity couldn't have imagined she'd be thinking about on Wednesday, June 12, 1974.

The seashore ended at a deep gully carved out by the crashing surf. Verity scrambled upwards on a rise of seagrass and sand, finding a comfortable spot to sit and observe. Beyond the cove was an impassable rock wall leading out to sea. The sea had become rough and looked angry now. The sand had been pushed to shore with fury, creating a sand drift and re-shaping the shoreline in spots. Large snail shells of golden yellow and brown were glued to the rocks. *A food source if the supply boat doesn't arrive on time*, Verity mused.

Rows of mussels made Verity's mouth water as she remembered a buttery sautéed appetizer served by Rick when he first had her over for dinner in their early days of dating. She smiled, remembering how they'd danced to Marvin Gaye's *Let's Get It On* while drinking Brandy Alexander's for dessert. She hoped he wasn't going crazy with her gone so far away but, true to form, he seemed to accept her felt need to get away. She somehow felt a measure of satisfaction knowing that he didn't have the cottage phone number. She would choose when/whether to give it to him. That was not to be mean or disrespectful, but Verity needed to feel her sense of agency now. She was in control, and she wanted to keep it that way.

She watched as the sea grew more turbulent. At times, the

receding wave crashed into the incoming, more aggressive wave, mitigating the shore-bound force. Other times, the receding wave blended in with the incoming wave, creating an even bigger crash.

As she studied the sea, Verity's eye was drawn to a bright yellow colour and shapes that resembled the head and the tail of a long, slender fish. It appeared to be struggling against the strength of the surf. Scurrying down off the rise, Verity repositioned herself for a better view. With her eyes glued to the floating object as it pitched and dove with the turbulence, Verity was determined to follow its journey. A strong incoming wave shot the object onto the shore where Verity could see a bright yellow plastic wrapping that likely once held something of use to the owner. She laughed inwardly at herself while simultaneously feeling the sharp incongruity of artificial material juxtaposed with this glorious natural setting.

A sudden movement to her left caught her attention: a massive splash of water erupted, followed by another, then a tapering off. Realizing she needed to keep a safe distance from the sea spray, Verity imagined the headline, 'Tourist swept into the sea at Tar Bay.' Reaching the end of the rock formation, she descended to the safety of ground level.

CHAPTER 3

Thursday, June 13, 1974

After a leisurely breakfast on her wrap-around veran-dah, Verity decided to turn left on her beach walk, heading north-west. When she reached the point where the shoreline veered inland toward the cottages and houses, a woman with long, platinum blond hair called out to her.

"Woohoo, hey there; do you have a minute?"

She was the first person Verity had seen on this pristine, empty beach. *Who is this person, and why is she calling out to me? How can I know it's safe to respond?* Yet, while Verity cherished the solitude, she also longed for human connection. Taking a chance, she shaded her eyes from the morning sun and turned toward the woman. They met halfway.

Verity smiled warmly. "Hello, I thought I was the only one here," she laughed.

"I know what you mean," the woman replied. "Isn't it heavenly? By the way, I'm Gina. There aren't many people walking the beach around here, so when I saw you, I thought I'd invite you in for a cold brew."

As they settled into two wicker chairs with blue-and-white-striped cushions, Gina served beer at 11:00 in the morning, and they began to chat.

"What brought you to Exuma?" Verity asked, genuinely interested.

Gina took a deep breath before sharing her story. "I came here to escape the life I knew," she began, her voice steady. "My mom was an alcoholic, and my dad was both a user and a dealer." She met Verity's gaze as if searching for empathy. "Mom passed away from liver failure when I was fourteen. With no family left, I ended up on the streets."

Verity's heart went out to Gina. "Oh, Gina, I'm so sorry. How old were you?"

"Seven, or at least I didn't become aware of what was going on until then. I didn't have a childhood. I couldn't bring friends over to our apartment. Can you imagine a kid walking into a place where their friend's dad is on a cocaine high? Or when he's delusional?"

Gina continued, her words flowing as if rehearsed. "I remember being paralyzed with fear one day when he burst into the apartment, screaming and cowering as if he were being chased by unseen threats." She laughed, the sound hollow, her eyes remaining distant.

Verity smiled faintly, sensing the depth of Gina's trauma. She recalled reading that humor could be a defense mechanism, a way to shield oneself from painful memories.

"At other times, he'd be so depressed he'd lie on a mattress on the floor in the middle of the afternoon, barely moving." Gina's expression darkened. "The apartment reeked of sweat and stale cigarette smoke, a combination that clung to everything. Yup, the nose never forgets, huh?"

Verity shook her head slowly, her heart heavy. "No life for a little girl."

Encouraged by Gina's openness, Verity asked, "What happened to you on the streets?"

Gina's lips curled into a wry smile. "I was young and, let's say, 'valuable' on the streets." She took a swig of her beer. "I became a significant earner for a man who ran several brothels in Miami."

Verity recoiled, her face reflecting her shock. "I can't fathom what you went through," she murmured. "When did you break free?"

"At eighteen," Gina replied, her eyes distant. "I ran for my life."

Verity leaned forward, her curiosity piqued. "How did you manage to escape?"

Gina's eyes darkened as she recalled her strategy. "I crafted a disguise—hat, sunglasses, oversized clothes—anything to hide my identity. I scavenged from the streets and beaches, piecing together what I could."

"And then?" Verity prompted.

"I chartered a boat to Nassau," Gina continued, her voice filled with pride. "Arriving in the Bahamas, free to start a new life, felt like a breath of fresh air." After a brief pause, Gina added, "Hell, it felt like being submerged in a tank of oxygen after gasping for air for so long."

Verity offered to fetch another beer, but Gina shook her head. "I think I need a joint," she joked. "Ah, never mind, I'm just kidding, hon," she added, perhaps sensing Verity's unease.

"Gina," Verity began gently, "your strength is inspiring. Thank you for sharing your story."

Gina shrugged. "It's my story. Part of who I am."

As they sat together, Verity felt a profound connection, grateful for the unexpected encounter that had brought them together.

"I got a job working as a chambermaid at a swanky hotel in downtown Nassau," Gina continued.

"Oh, that'd be quite a change of scene," Verity acknowledged.

"Indeed. Luxury bedding, plush carpets, complimentary wine, people dressed in fancy clothes. Porters. Valets. Yes, it was a different world, all right." Gina glanced at her modest furnishings and then shifted her gaze to the large picture window framing her ocean view. "This ain't bad either," she said proudly.

"Looks like you've done very well for yourself, Gina. I'm proud of you." Verity noticed a hint of discomfort cross Gina's face at the praise. It seemed that compliments were either unfamiliar or unsettling for her.

Verity stretched her arms high over her head before resting them in her lap, signaling she was ready for the rest of the story. "Please, go on," she said, her eyes warm and encouraging.

Gina forged ahead. "So, to continue... One morning, I knocked on a hotel room door, calling out that it was housekeeping. No one answered, and there was no 'Do Not Disturb' sign, so I unlocked the door and stepped inside."

"Oh, man, Gina, I'm on the edge of my seat," Verity joked.

Gina tilted her head, offering a crooked smile. "He was twenty-five—the same age I am now. And he was gorgeous. Well-dressed. Lots of moolah."

"Let me guess," Verity said. "This was your future husband?"

Gina laughed. "You guessed it—but not for long. And that turned out to be a good thing for two reasons."

She counted on her fingers, glancing up at Verity. "One, he was a wife-beater. Two, the divorce was finalized just three weeks before a legal firm tracked me down with some good news. No surprise—Dad hadn't left a will. But by law, I was the sole heir to his fortune."

Her grin widened. "I quit my job that same day."

Gina took a drag on her cigarette, exhaling with satisfaction.

Verity sat quietly for a moment, then smiled. "That's an amazing story, Gina. Thanks for sharing it." She stretched her hands out to the side, palms up, and motioned around the room. "And after all that, you ended up here. Maybe this is your happy ending."

Gina returned the smile and headed toward the fridge. She cracked open another beer. "Care for another, Verity?"

"Sure, thanks," Verity said, not wanting to leave abruptly after Gina had shared such a gut-wrenching story. She took a sip of her beer, her mind drifting back to Vancouver and her time teaching at Hillside College. She'd been known for her particular empathy toward students from disadvantaged backgrounds, those who faced tough life challenges. Sometimes, adding a program of study on top of all that was enough to tip the balance in the wrong direction. Verity had become an advocate for some, trying to convince the higher-ups that these students were worthy, that they deserved a second chance—even if they arrived to class with the smell of alcohol on their breath.

Hearing Gina's story sparked Verity's empathetic nature, and since Gina was eager to share, Verity wanted to contribute to the conversation in the best way she knew how.

"So, you came here to refresh your soul, to give yourself a chance to rejuvenate? I can relate to that. It's exactly what I'm doing here, though my story doesn't compare to yours."

"Well, that's good, Verity. I wouldn't wish my former life on anyone, but I know my story is far from unique."

"Sad but true, Gina. And of course, we can't undo the past." Verity paused for a moment, watching Gina shrug her shoulders. "But when we turn a new page, we can do so with the benefit of learning a few things from our past. Don't you think?"

Gina smirked, raising her eyebrows as if to say, *Go on.*

"You know what I like, Gina?" Verity sensed she was pushing it, but couldn't stop herself.

"Mm, maybe a Moscow mule right about now?"

Verity ignored the thought that Gina might be making fun of her.

"What I like is that we have the luxury of free will. Even though the choices we make in life shape our trajectory, our path forward, we still can change it."

"Yeah, I know what you mean. That's why I moved away from all that crap."

"Thank goodness you did, Gina. I imagine there are a lot of people who want to move on but don't know how. It takes a different kind of strength, I guess—a certain kind of confidence."

"Or maybe just running blindly at full speed in the opposite direction. I knew I had nothing to lose unless they caught up with me. I figured that whatever I found, it had to be better than this."

"You were so brave, Gina."

"Having a plan helped; it sustained me. Otherwise, I'd have had no hope."

"Yes, I can see that. Your mindset allowed you to see the possibility of a positive outcome."

"Uh-huh. And where did I get that?" Gina's guttural laugh, rough and raspy, made Verity wonder if she'd been smoking for a long time.

"Right. I think you were the exception for people in your circumstances. I believe our hearts close up when they get overloaded with too much stress. And when that happens, we block out even the good things in life. Even the good people. They might be trying to help us restore and show us a different path, but if our hearts aren't open, well-intentioned messages aren't getting through."

"Ha, well, I'll tell ya, darlin'," Gina said, crossing her legs, "there seemed to be a severe shortage of good people back in the day." She took a drag on her cigarette, carefully blowing the smoke away from Verity.

"I can only imagine, Gina. And I don't want to sound preachy, believe me, but in my experience, when it feels like no one's around to love you, you have to learn to love yourself."

Gina took another swig of beer and butted out her cigarette. "Yeah, that 'love yourself' shit never did sound very appealing to me. Maybe to the hippies. I mean, I guess, I just think that if you don't have even one other person in this entire world to love you, then why bother loving yourself?"

Heading to the kitchen to get a glass of water, Verity briefly touched the back of Gina's shoulder. "Please know that you are worthy, Gina; I know you're worthy."

"Ha, nice try, Ver, but we don't really know each other." Gina's anger seemed to hover just below the surface, Verity thought. *Maybe behind that tough exterior is a person who's just as scared and* Sitting back down in the wicker chair, Verity couldn't argue with Gina's reaction. But having struggled with feelings of worthlessness for much of her own life, she understood, to some degree. She tried again. "It's just that I think, in order to unburden our souls and reopen our hearts, we have to start by being kind to ourselves."

Since Gina was still listening, not taking her eyes off Verity and not interrupting, Verity continued. "When we begin to take care of our own needs, we start setting boundaries. We begin to say 'No' to things that aren't good for us. We stop letting people take advantage of us or treat us poorly."

"Yeah, I do tend to kybosh myself, I'll admit that," Gina allowed, shifting in her seat.

Verity sensed she was nearing the edge of Gina's tolerance for advice. "Hey, I hope you know I'm not criticizing you, Gina, far from it. You've had a tough life, no question, and I just wanted to say I empathize with your situation and congratulate you for making a change. I've made changes myself, and I'm hoping to unburden my heart, too."

"What's made your heart so heavy, hon?" Gina brightened, probably relieved to shift the focus off herself and onto Verity.

Not wanting to dwell on the past herself, Verity skirted the question. "You know, I came here to forget. Part of my rebuild is soaking up this beautiful new world. Here, I have no one to answer to, no schedules to keep, no responsibilities other than those any of us have to the world community, shall we say?" *She's going to cringe at the 'world community' phrase, I'm sure.* "But for now, I'm learning to shed my worries, open my mind to new experiences, and connect with nature."

"Sounds like a plan, Ver." Rising from her chair, Gina added, "Now, if you don't mind, I've got to see a man about a dog. So, I'll say Sayonara for now. Thanks for the visit, dear." She smiled at Verity, who suddenly felt a bit foolish.

As Verity descended the stone steps, she inwardly scoffed at Gina's terms of endearment, which felt like arrows of condescension. *I'm not your dear, your hon, your darlin'. You don't even know me.*

By the time she stood at the shore, staring out at the sea and trying to process her visit with Gina, she conceded that she had, in fact, feigned familiarity when she'd told Gina she was "worthy." She'd passed judgment on someone she barely knew.

Continuing her beach walk, Verity reflected on her idea of being 'free.' *It's just not possible to leave all your responsibilities behind, even if you're on vacation. My heart won't let me ignore pain when I see it. And I can easily see the pain in Gina's heart.*

She kicked the sand with her feet, wondering what might lie beneath. She popped as many air bladders as she could find on seaweed shoved about by the tide. *There's the responsibility to yourself and others, not just in your local community but in the global community too.*

She stooped down and picked up an empty can of beer, laughing to herself. *There's no vacation from being a good citizen of the world, but I need a break from trying to save people who don't want to be saved.*

After a few moments, Verity had a good talk with herself. *You had no business offering unasked-for advice to Gina. She opened up to you, and you made judgments. Sure, she's smoking, drinking, and maybe even doing drugs, but that's her business, not yours.*

CHAPTER 4

Friday, June 14 – 21, 1974

From now on, Verity kept her head tilted forward during beach walks, her eyes darting as she scanned the sand for seashells. She planned to make her own seashell lamp when she returned to Vancouver, inspired by the one in the cottage living room. Occasionally, she glanced ahead, hoping to spot an exotic shell before anyone else could claim it—not that there seemed to be anyone else around. But still.

She searched for multiple shells of the same kind to form the lamp's base, just as the cottage lamp had been designed. The shiny, white, fan-shaped domes, resembling tiny lightbulbs, were plentiful and often whole. Clamshells, sturdier and abundant, added texture to her collection with their ridged surfaces, each groove catching the light. She was particularly drawn to the ones tinged with rust, their earthy warmth breaking up the expanse of white.

Orange shells proved harder to find, but when scattered among the neutrals, they added an unexpected brightness, a kind of secret warmth. Some days, Verity gathered handfuls of sunray venus shells

—elongated ovals streaked with pink and gold, their colours reminiscent of a vibrant sunset. Occasionally, she even found doubles. Opening them required a delicate touch to keep both halves intact. When she spread them wide and held them up to the light, they looked like butterflies. *Butterflies of the sea.*

She often consulted the shell guidebook she'd picked up in Georgetown, flipping through its pages each morning before heading out. The best finds, she figured, would have been scattered along the shore overnight, waiting to be discovered.

A week into her routine, Verity was rewarded with something new—a conch, unlike the creamy beige ones she and her childhood friends had pressed to their ears, listening for sounds of the sea. This one was different. Smaller. Its central spiral lay exposed as if the outer shell had been peeled away, revealing an iridescent pale blue core with a silvery sheen. She turned it in her hand, admiring how the sunlight skimmed its surface. Shelling had become more than a pastime; it settled her, grounding her in the simple joys of her new surroundings.

She walked on, turning this way and that, even nudging apart clumps of seagrass in search of hidden treasures. Up ahead, something caught her eye—a flash of turquoise blue. She quickened her pace. It was a fan-shaped shell, smooth and perfect, unlike any she had seen in her guidebook. Bending down, she reached for it, lifting it into her palm. Light. Too light. The moment she held it up to the sun, she realized—plastic.

She let out a breath, half amusement, half disappointment, and tossed the imposter aside.

Her stomach rumbled, breaking the quiet. Time to head back. But today, instead of lunch at Casuarina House, she craved a change of scenery. Maybe she'd try out the George Café and poke around the marina for a bit.

Slipping on her red leather sandals, she took a moment to savor the smell of new leather, and the stiffness of the straps as she threaded them through the buckle. A small pleasure, but a satisfying one. She felt like a little girl again, giddy over a fresh pair of shoes.

Skipping makeup, she grabbed a bottle of water for the drive and stepped out the door, ready to explore.

CHAPTER 5

Friday, June 21

Driving along the Queen's Highway in the daylight, Verity noticed the asphalt's edges were jagged and crumbling. In some places, it was so badly worn away that she had to veer into the right lane, carefully checking for oncoming traffic around a dangerous curve. The road was narrow, and when a large truck came barrelling toward her, she was forced to drive on the shoulder. A motorcyclist came by, travelling in the opposite direction as he took a swig from a cola bottle. Glancing in her rear-view mirror as he roared by, she saw him toss the empty bottle into the ditch.

In Georgetown, Verity found a parking spot directly in front of George's Café. Even though it was Friday and the grocery store would likely be crowded, she was a bit ahead of the lunch hour, although she didn't yet have a feel for what Friday noon would look like in Georgetown.

Looking out her car window at the rustic café with its weathered boards and a driftwood sign out front, Verity could see an array of painted metal fish hanging across the two large front windows and a young couple sitting in front of the window to the left. Next to the café stood Lacey J's Gift Shop, and Verity planned to wander over there after lunch.

As Verity pressed the door handle and swung open the door of George's Café, a string of bells attached to the door handle inside announced her presence. Taking the remaining window seat, she set her purse down on the floor and settled into her chair just as a man who looked to be in his late twenties walked toward her table.

"Hi, there," he said with a smile, "would you like a menu?"

Verity hadn't expected to be stunned by her server, but there was no ignoring his looks.

"Uh, sure," she smiled back, looking directly into the deepest blue eyes she had ever seen. His thick, wavy black hair tempted Verity to imagine running her fingers through it, down to the bare skin of his neck. She glanced down at her purse, hoping he wasn't a mind reader. *Or maybe I hope he is.*

Mr. Gorgeous set the menu down on the table and, still smiling, said, "Take your time," in a deep, buttery-smooth voice. As he turned and walked toward the counter, Verity shifted in her chair and picked up the paper menu. It took her a moment to focus on the words as she tried to sort out what had just happened. Her reaction. After all, she didn't embark on this getaway looking for a man. Rick was waiting for her at home in Vancouver. *Okay, so I'm attracted to this guy; so what? I came here to just be, and here I am just being.*

The jangling of bells caused Verity to look up from the menu as two women wearing colourful, short shifts and heavy makeup entered the café. "Hi, Rylan," they chirped musically like two purple finches on a telephone wire. Grinning widely, they walked toward Rylan as if he were the special of the day.

Verity's eyes were glued to the scene as her man Rylan stooped down and greeted each woman with a kiss on the cheek. "Hey, long time no see, ladies; where've you been?"

The one wearing a bright orange shift glanced at the other woman and then, laughing, back to Rylan. "Oh, wouldn't you like to know?" she teased.

"As a matter of fact, Janesta, I *would* like to know." Noticing Verity setting her menu aside, he continued, "But, excuse me for a moment, lovelies, I have a customer..." and off he went to attend to Verity.

As Rylan approached, Verity slid the menu closer again, confirming her choice with one last glance. She looked up at Rylan, smiling with her eyes and lips. "Yes, I'd like the crab salad, please."

"Anything to drink?" Verity noticed his right brow lifting as he asked. Rylan stood there, all charm and confidence as if he could grant her every wish. What she could see of his muscular form fuelled her curiosity to know what was underneath those denim shorts and white tee.

"Just some ice water with a slice of lemon, if you have it, please."

"Is lime okay?"

"Lime's fine," Verity smiled, sitting back in her chair and observing Rylan as she handed him the menu. *Anything's fine, Rylan.* In Verity's mind, she and Rylan were the only two people in the room until they were distracted by the noisy chatter and giggling of the two female strangers waiting in the wings.

"My pleasure. I'll get your water right away." Returning to the two women, Rylan said, "You know, it's going to get pretty busy here real quick, so how 'bout we meet for drinks after work, and we can catch up then? Would that suit you both?"

"Great," replied the woman in the pink shift. "See you at the Plenty around six?"

"Perfect." Rylan winked at them. "Lookin' forward to it; it's been far too long." They waved and smiled as they skipped out of the café just as cheerily as they'd entered.

The bells jangled as they shut the door behind them, and Rylan disappeared into the back. Moments later, he returned with a tall glass of ice water garnished with a wedge of lime.

"Oh, that looks awesome. I'm not used to this heat," Verity announced to Rylan as he set the glass down on her table.

Rylan paused as if wanting to join Verity in conversation. He stood back a bit, making it easier to see her from his height. "Where're you from?" he asked softly, casting his stunning blue eyes over Verity's as though sizing up the situation.

"Vancouver, Canada. Ever been there?" She invited his conversation, keeping her smiling eyes steady on his.

"Once. If I had to live in a city, then waterfront would be my choice," he said agreeably.

"Oh, spoken like a true islander, I guess." Verity quickly brought the focus back to Rylan.

Rylan laughed. "You might say that. I'm not the big-city type, that's for sure," he smiled. "I'll be right back with your salad."

Verity squeezed lime juice into her glass and tossed in the rest of the wedge. Taking a drink of the ice-cold water, she heard a familiar song in the background, *Sloop John B*, but this was not The Beach Boys' recording she knew. She was still tapping her foot when Rylan returned with the salad.

"Hey, that's a different version of *Sloop John B*," she stated, hoping to engage Rylan in further conversation.

He grinned and said, "That's right. Here you're more likely to hear the recording by the Dicey Doh Singers. This one's from the album *Bahamas: Islands of Song*."

"How interesting and, oh, that salad looks delicious," Verity exclaimed, hoping she didn't sound too eager to please.

"Good; I hope you enjoy it." Rylan glanced toward the door as it jangled open again, but Verity kept her eyes on Rylan instead.

"Hey, Buzzy! How's it goin'?" asked Rylan.

Rylan welcomed his friend, placing his left arm across Buzzy's shoulders. As they conversed, Verity took a bite of her salad, savoring the mix of citrusy, fresh island crab with crispy iceberg lettuce. *Seems like Rylan's well-liked; no surprise there.*

When it was time for the bill, Rylan asked Verity to pay at the counter when she was ready. Grabbing her purse off the floor, Verity stepped up to the counter, grateful that there was a lull in customers coming and going. "That salad was to die for, Rylan...Oh, I hope you don't mind me calling you Rylan," she said, and she could feel a rising warmth in her cheeks.

Rylan chuckled, "Not at all. I guess you heard my name a few times while sitting there. You can hear every word in this place." *I could listen to that voice all day long.* Rylan's eyes smiled as Verity handed him her credit card.

"By the way, what's your name?" They held each other's gaze and, just in that second, a spark ignited in Verity's inner psyche. *Oh, how I'd like to spend more time with this man.*

"Verity." She extended her hand and focussed on the skin-to-skin connection as she smiled her sweetest smile and said, "Pleased to meet you, Rylan."

"Have you ever had a conch salad?" he asked as he tore her receipt off the machine.

"Conch? No, I haven't; is it good?"

"Yes, do you like ceviche?"

"I'm not big on raw fish," she replied. "I read an article once about health concerns regarding eating uncooked fish."

"Yes, I understand, but it's the Bahamian ceviche, so it's not actually raw. The citrus juice cooks the fish."

"Well, if you say...." Verity was sure that her eyes looked playful.

"I do say and, if you want to try it sometime, I'd be happy to show you how it's done."

"Sounds fabulous, Rylan. I'd love to." Verity's eyes widened as she looked at him, waiting for more details.

"If you give me your number, I'll let you know when I'm free."

Verity hesitated. "Oh... I didn't take note of my cottage number."

Rylan laughed, "Did you just arrive in Exuma?"

"Yes, got in late on Tuesday. "

"Where're you staying?"

"Casuarina House."

Rylan's eyes lit up, both brows raised. "I know exactly where you are. How 'bout I drop by on Sunday? The café's closed, so I could be there around, let's say tenish?"

"It's a date," Verity ventured, unsure if she was a bit too forward.

"A date it is, Verity. See you on Sunday."

Rylan smiled, this time showing his teeth, perfectly straight and white, and a pair of dimples that caused Verity to question her decision not to wear any makeup that day.

Turning the ignition in the Vauxhall, Verity reasoned, *He seems to like me as I am, so I'm going with that.* She'd completely forgotten that she'd planned to visit the shop next door called Lacey J's.

CHAPTER 6

At 9:12 a.m., there was barely a breeze on the verandah. Just like night turning into day, Verity's concerns about a possible hurricane had disappeared. This morning's thoughts were far lighter —like the delicious-looking Rylan, who sent a flutter through her stomach. She was still surprised that she'd landed a date with a charismatic stranger who seemed well-liked—at least by the patrons of George's Café. Dating hadn't even been on her radar, yet here she was, six days into her vacation, with a date lined up.

Verity checked her watch when, at 9:55, she heard the roar of a motorcycle on the main road, then detected it slowing to come down her driveway. She walked to the part of the verandah facing her visitor and waved cheerily at Rylan. "Right on time," she acknowledged, then made her way down the back steps of the verandah and walked toward his motorcycle.

"I'm not known for my tardiness. Comes from being a café owner for about ten years now." The Rylan Verity saw that morning was the same Rylan she saw now. It wasn't like buying a dress you thought you loved on Saturday, then returning it on Sunday because you'd misjudged.

"Wait—you own George's Café? How did that happen?"

Rylan engaged the kickstand on his bike and walked toward Verity. "I was in the inheritance business, I guess you'd say. Not from my family, but from the guy who opened the original George's back in 1935."

"Oh, wow, it's been there that long."

"Yep, Jed ran the café for twenty-nine years until he died at the age of sixty-four."

"That's young; was he sick?"

"Stage four melanoma by the time he was diagnosed." Rylan looked down at the ground. After a few more steps, he stopped walking, facing the beach. "I'd forgotten what a fantastic view you get from here."

"Oh, you've been here before, then?"

"Oh, yes, Casuarina House has seen a lot of visitors in its sixty-four-year history. But none as enigmatic as Endolyn Crowe. She was the last renter of the cottage until it sold three years ago. And she had kind of an 'open-door policy,' allowing visitors near and far to come and party at her place."

Verity wrinkled her forehead. "I'm surprised. That is, uh, well, I guess that so far, I don't really see Exuma as being a party town."

Rylan laughed. "It's not; that's for sure. But now, the party comes to the bay in the form of a party boat out of Nassau. Sure, there's a lot of retirees here, but after you've spent some time on the island, things might look a little different."

Rylan sat down on the front steps and said, "Why don't we take a walk on the beach?" He removed his shoes and socks and headed barefoot across the carpet of long brown needles. Then, turning toward Verity, he asked, "May I?" as he joined his right hand with hers, and they headed toward the powdery sand. *Oh, and he's polite and considerate on top of being a hunk.*

Like I was going to refuse, Verity smiled to herself. "By the way, Rylan, do you happen to know the name of those trees right there, the ones with the long needles that look like the vanes of a feather?"

"Those are casuarina trees, indigenous to the island," he said, motioning her toward the northeast, an area she had yet to explore.

"Oh, thus the name *Casuarina House*," she laughed.

"So, tell me about yourself, Verity. What did you do back in Vancouver?"

"I taught at a community college." She paused. "But, you know, I came here to leave all of that behind. I'm looking at that as another lifetime." Another pause. "I'm here to begin anew and, frankly, to get to know myself better."

"Uh-huh," Rylan replied, nodding his head. "It's always good to know yourself well, to know what you value in life."

Validation. Not that she needed it, Verity told herself—but she appreciated that Rylan listened. Feeling comfortable, Verity continued as they walked along the beach. "You know, Rylan, I thought I knew my values frontward and backward, sideways and upside down. And I was naïve to think that others shared the same values as I did, as if that mattered."

"Oh, sounds like this conversation is turning far too heavy. Let me see if I can catapult you out of that frame of mind." Rylan began to nudge Verity sideways toward the water. Laughing, Verity pushed back but without much consequence other than to find herself stepping awkwardly into the water, hoping not to lose her flip-flops. Rylan turned her to face the incoming surf, gently moving her forward bit by bit.

Laughing, Verity tried to resist, but the shifting sand betrayed her. She stumbled into the shallows, instinctively grasping Rylan for balance. His broad shoulders, the solid warmth of his body—yeah, she'd almost forgotten how good it felt to be close to a man.

One flip-flop floated up to the surface and was beginning to drift away. Rylan lurched forward and grabbed it while Verity removed the other one and headed back to shore.

"Okay, you win, Verity, but know that this story is to be continued." The glint in his eye vaguely reminded her of the glassy eye of the barracuda she encountered on her first day in Exuma.

Hand-in-hand, they walked back to the sandy shore and continued their walk. Verity loved seeing the fun side of Rylan and his relaxed manner. *He's so easy to be with.*

No one else on the beach so far. The motion of a diving bird drew Verity's attention to the right. At first, she thought of a kingfisher, but this bird was a lot larger. The underside and head were mostly white. "What's that bird, do you know?"

Rylan glanced in the direction Verity pointed and said, "Yes, looks like an osprey."

"Oh, I've never seen an osprey before," Verity was as excited as a child seeing an owl for the first time. "I'll tell you, Rylan, I'm a real nature lover, and I can't wait to meet the flora and fauna of the Bahamas."

The way Rylan smiled told her he liked that. Maybe they had that in common.

Rylan lightened things up again, giving Verity the impression that he liked to play. "Oh, you'll find all kinds of wildlife on this island, Verity," and he laughed at his own joke. *Take me away, Rylan.*

As they approached an area of low rock and grass among the sand, Verity was glad to be wearing her flip-flops. Rylan walked on, undeterred, saying he was "an island boy" and that the soles of his feet were thick as canvas. They'd passed a few cottages on the left, but when they approached Gina's cottage with its stone facing, Verity stopped, not mentioning that she'd already been inside. "Fieldstone. That almost looks out of place here."

Even though Verity had been inside already, her meeting with Gina happened too fast for her to take in the cottage exterior. When she first was summoned by Gina's friendly welcome, her focus was more on questions such as 'Why is this stranger calling after me?' and 'Is it safe to engage when there's no one around if I need help?'

There were stone steps up to the front door set in a semi-circular fashion, and the front door was slightly ajar. A lime green watering can had been placed on the landing. Pots of coral-coloured geraniums were placed on the steps, spilling out onto the edge of the property, indicating that the cottage was occupied. *No squatters allowed here.* A sheer white dress, illuminated by the sun, hung on the clothesline. Having already met Gina, Verity now felt the incongruity of the romantic cottage setting with the unfiltered, crusty personality of the owner.

Rylan glanced at the house, then turned to look at the rising tide. "Almost as out of place as the owner," he mused.

Verity's forehead creased as she looked up at Rylan. "So, you know Gina, then?"

"Yes. Endolyn Crowe, known locally as Gina. I mentioned her as the last renter of Casuarina House before you. It seems she prefers to live her life in seclusion, even though she lives right here on the beach." He paused and then seemed to contradict himself. "Well, no, she does make a point of coming on the party boat now and then."

Verity laughed. "Yes, but this is Tar Bay and, from what I've seen, it's not exactly Grand Central Station. How do you know Gina?"

"Oh, she used to be quite the party girl. You know, back in the day when Casuarina House actually was like Grand Central Station." Rylan's dimples and the intense blue of his eyes against the backdrop of the sea distracted Verity for a moment.

"I'm intrigued." Verity raised her brows to full height. Rylan removed his shirt, revealing a hairless chest and a tattoo behind his right shoulder in the shape of a starfish.

Rylan pulled Verity toward the water again. "C'mon, what say we cool ourselves off a bit? That sun's getting pretty hot."

Verity paused to remove her flip-flops and toss them well up on the shore. She pulled her tee over her head and removed her pull-on shorts, happy she'd worn her bikini today. Hand-in-hand, they continued until the water tickled Verity's waist. She released Rylan's hand and swam into the incoming wave, riding high with the rise and easing down with the fall. Rylan joined her in riding the waves, keeping enough distance from Verity to avoid a crash.

The water was warm, and billowy white clouds filtered the hot sun, making it a perfect day for playing in the surf. "Ouch." Verity instinctively leaned forward looking down into the water as a sharp, piercing pain shot up her big toe. She limped toward shore so she could assess the damage.

"Are you okay?" Rylan shouted from a short distance above the sound of the waves.

"Yes, I should've worn my water shoes," she said with a grimace. Once ashore, Verity massaged her toe and put her flip-flops back on. Just then, her attention was diverted to the door of the stone cottage slamming shut. Looking up, she could see a dark figure passing by the white-paned windows and disappearing from view.

"Hmm, someone's not happy," she said to Rylan as he stepped in from the sea.

"Why do you say that?"

"I guess the slamming of the door competed with the sound of the surf but, I'm telling you, that was one forceful slam."

Rylan's shorts were dripping wet. Using his tee-shirt as a towel, he dried off what he could. Verity followed his queue with her own tee and squeezed the excess water from her long brown hair.

When Rylan didn't respond, Verity said, "Shall we head back? I can make us some lunch. Maybe you can show me how to make conch salad another day." Verity picked up her wet shorts and joined them with her wet tee. "Besides, I forgot my hat and need to get into some shade."

"I'd love to spend the afternoon with you, Verity, but I can't." Rylan took her hand as they headed back toward the cottage. "A friend of mine has offered to groom my dog today, so I have to get Prints to her by two this aft."

"Oh, you have a dog called Prince. What kind of dog?"

"He's a black lab and, just in case you think it's a royal title, it's not. It's spelled p-r-i-n-t-s, as in paw prints."

Verity chuckled at the clever name. "I hope I get to meet him; black labs are awesome." Then she imagined Prints on the motorcycle. "How'll you transport Prints to the groomer?" she asked with a few mild creases on her forehead.

"I have a beater pickup truck in the garage. It's pretty much a necessity for transporting supplies, equipment, and yes, Prints around the island." Rylan found his socks and runners near his motorcycle, grabbed a dry pair of shorts and tee from a storage bag, and asked Verity if he could use her outdoor shower.

"Of course; I'll get you some towels."

The outdoor shower was just that, a shower in the open right beside the verandah. No stall. It was far enough away from the beach that a curious onlooker would have to use binoculars to get a good view.

Verity draped two plush, yellow-striped towels over the verandah railing, within easy reach of Rylan. Although she caught a glimpse of him in the nude as he was soaping himself, one arm up in the air, he was facing away from the cottage, so she saw only the rear view. But still. She fought the urge to strip off her bikini and join him. Instead, she moved away to her morning coffee site and waited for him to finish.

"How was that?" she asked as he emerged from the shower looking fresh and satisfied, his wet dark hair stirring her imagination. He swept the hair out of his eyes, slicking it back into an even more enticing, sexy beach look.

"Nice. Perfect. I love outdoor showers. Have you tried it yet?" Rylan smiled with a gleam in his eye.

"Next on my list," Verity said, drawing a checkmark in the air and laughing in her eyes.

"Maybe we can shower together next time," The glint of playfulness in Rylan's eyes sparkled like that momentary glint from a diamond when the light hits it just right.

"You should be so lucky," Verity said, not wanting Rylan to make any foregone conclusions. She would continue to play it cool, not giving too much away, and she hoped he wouldn't be presumptuous about their beginnings. But she knew for sure that she did want this to be the beginning of a relationship. *How else can I know if Rick is right for me?*

Verity's instincts told her that this could be an important relationship. Her biggest dream was that it could be nourished into something wonderful, something to treasure and never let go. *But I'm getting way ahead of myself.*

When they were together by his motorcycle, Rylan wrapped one arm around Verity's waist. "If you like, I could stop by this eve..." He looked tentatively at Verity, who paused as if considering her response.

Verity smiled, not wanting to look too eager but knowing she would like nothing more. "Oh, hey, let me give you my phone number, now that I know what it is. I can write it down for you..."

Reaching back to his storage bag, Rylan said, "Just a sec; I have a pen and paper here." Verity wondered if he kept that handy for the many other times he might have occasion to write down phone numbers of other women. *Don't be so insecure; you have no real reason to be suspicious. Besides, you don't own this gorgeous hunk of man.*

She provided the number and asked, "Any idea of what time you might come by tonight?" Verity's former self might have raised one shoulder and tilted her head to the right. She resisted doing that now. No, this was just a practical question. She wasn't desperate, after all, she already had a boyfriend in Vancouver, and he was a keeper as far as she knew. *But we're not married, we're 5,000 km away, and I intend to live my life.*

"Let's say around seven. I'll bring a bottle of bubbly to celebrate our having met; how does that sound?" Rylan brushed his lips against her cheek so lightly as to tickle.

Verity giggled, happy that he seemed to consider their meeting a celebratory occasion. "Sounds more than wonderful, Rylan. See you later, and drive safely. I'm not so sure about the roads around here."

"I grew up here, babe. There are few surprises for me, but thanks for the concern." With a kickstart of the motor, Rylan leaned over to give a quick kiss to Verity's lips, and headed out the driveway.

He called me 'babe'; he's bringing champagne; this guy moves fast. Listening to the buzz of his motorcycle as Rylan pulled onto the Queen's Highway, Verity missed him already.

CHAPTER 7

Seven o'clock arrived quickly. Verity had driven to Georgetown to pick up an assortment of hors d'oeuvres; thankfully, the shelves had been restocked. She'd changed the sheets on her bed, too, just in case.

Watching Rylan ascend the three steps to the cottage, carrying a bottle of champagne, she assumed, Verity admired how good he looked in his clothes and already had a pretty good idea of how he looked without them. *Don't get ahead of yourself.*

"Let's put this in the fridge for a bit to make sure it's properly chilled before serving, okay?" Without waiting for an answer, Rylan headed to the fridge, opened the door, and placed the bottle inside. "Oh, that looks good," Rylan said, seeing the plate of shrimp with asparagus tips and slices of lemon and bread. "Celebratory food for a celebratory evening."

Verity's lips curled into a deep smile as she joined him near the fridge, lightly touching the back of his left shoulder, resting it there for just a moment. "I thought we'd sit out on the verandah and watch the sunset; how's that sound?"

47

"Sounds great," said Rylan, "but you do know about the no-see-ums, right?"

"Huh? You mean those minuscule bitey/pinchy bugs that attack you before you know it and cause you to scratch your skin raw because the itch won't go away? Aka midges?"

"Yes. So, we either cover ourselves in bug spray or make sure that no skin is showing unless, of course, you have a candle repellant."

"Do they even work? I think I saw something like that in the kitchen drawer. I'll go check."

Verity retrieved the package she'd spotted earlier. "Ah, here it is. Lemongrass is effective against midges. Let's give it a whirl."

Verity set six candles around the verandah railings and another on the table between the Adirondacks on the back verandah. The gentle breeze made the flames flicker but wasn't strong enough to snuff them out. The night air was invitingly warm, with still about an hour until sunset.

Rylan stood, gazing toward the ocean, and Verity couldn't help but admire the delicious contrast of his broad shoulders and narrow waist. "Hey, would you like me to mix up some margaritas?"

"Oh, sounds perfect for a warm summer evening spent with a beautiful woman alone in a strange land," he teased. "May I have mine on the rocks?"

"You know what, Rylan? I have to say that I just love your polite and thoughtful manner. Are you like that with all women?" Verity reconsidered her question, thinking it was stupid. *What's he gonna say, 'No, I'm only like that with you?'*

"I had a good role model," smiled Rylan. Verity assumed it was his father.

She headed into the kitchen. One of the first things Verity had noticed that first morning in the cottage was a row of six cocktail glasses lined up on a wooden shelf under the kitchen cupboards. Each had a quirky green cactus stem. Like the painting of colourful parrots by the dining table, they added a festive vibe to her new surroundings.

Verity served chips and salsa with the margaritas set on the wooden table between the two red Adirondacks. The lapping of waves as they reached the shore washed over Verity as she nestled into her chair. The peace and happiness she felt sitting there with Rylan together alone in this island paradise were exactly what she'd hoped to experience when she left Vancouver, completely depleted. That she would find it so quickly was beyond her wildest imaginings.

"So, what do you do for fun besides date women who rent cottages for the short term?" Verity's eyes looked mischievous as she placed one hand on Rylan's left forearm and leaned forward, twisting to look into his eyes.

"Ha! So that's the impression I've given you, is it? You think I'm a womanizer?" Rylan jerked back in his chair as if he'd just heard something incredulous, then his dimples revealed his enjoyment of Verity's sleuthing behavior. "Sure," he laughed, "I won't deny that I do enjoy the occasional fling; what man wouldn't? But...your question seems to imply something more." He looked at Verity expectantly.

Verity cleared her throat and took another sip of her margarita. "I don't know, Rylan," she tried to choose her words carefully. "My impression is that you're quite popular with the ladies, I mean, just judging by the welcome party of two who walked into your café on Friday while I was there."

Rylan thought for a moment. "Oh, haha, you're talking about Cassie and Janesta." He glanced downward momentarily, then tilted his head back as if looking at the stars, even though it was still too early for stars. "Party girls from the party boat."

"Hmm, I guess I'll have to check out this party boat. What d'you think?"

"Sure, comes by every Friday during the summer. It's a lot of fun. Gives the young and the young-at-heart something to look forward to in Sleepy Town. Maybe we can go together sometime if you want. Docks right here in Tar Bay."

"Woah, action right here at my backyard ocean. Who knew?"

Verity loved that she and Rylan seemed to share a sense of fun. She'd had to be so serious back in Vancouver, and it felt good to unleash the 'little girl' side of her now.

She could feel the dulling effects of the alcohol already, not having indulged in anything other than a glass of wine with dinner since her arrival. *Take it easy, don't drink too much. Keep your wits about you.* She walked into the kitchen and came back with the plate of shrimp and asparagus tips.

With the scent of lemongrass in the air, Rylan popped the champagne cork using his hand to prevent it from flying up into the rafters. Verity had chilled two champagne flutes, surprised that the cottage was equipped with a variety of glassware.

Rylan skillfully poured champagne into both flutes, tipped his glass toward Verity's, and looked directly into her eyes. "Cheers, babe."

"Cheers," she said, taking a sip of bubbly and savoring the cool lightness and the delicious ambiance of their rendezvous. They stood side by side looking out to sea.

With the evening progressing, the night sky was lit by a full moon and a thousand twinkling stars, making the foaming, white surf visible in the distance.

As they nibbled away at hor d'ouerves, Verity asked, "And just what kind of parties went on here in my peaceful little haven?"

"I'd say it was an 'anything goes' kind of atmosphere. Some people dressed up in costume, and some wore nothing at all, which was handy for all the nude swimming that went on. Do you like to swim in the nude?" Rylan leaned in close to Verity, eyebrows raised.

Verity didn't want to sound like a prude, but she was honest. "No, actually, I haven't, but..."

Rylan grabbed that thought. "You know, it's warm enough tonight that we could make this a 'first' for you unless you're adverse to my good company..."

Verity smiled at the suggestion, considering it. She took another sip of champagne, making it easier to make her decision. "Can't say that I haven't wanted to try, Rylan, and maybe this is a perfect time. I don't want to swim alone, especially at night."

"You're on," Rylan said, twisting it around to make it seem like it was Verity's idea in the first place.

"Just a moment, I'll just get rid of these cumbersome clothes," Verity joked, sliding open the screen door to her bedroom just off the verandah. Looking back at Rylan, she said, "I'll get you a towel."

"No need," said Rylan, removing a large beach towel from the clothesline and already unbuttoning his shorts. "Towels dry out real fast in this climate."

When Verity emerged from her bedroom, she had only a striped, orange towel wrapped around her body. She caught her hair up in a clip and slipped into her flip-flops.

She giggled down the slope toward the water, one hand in Rylan's and the other securing her towel. Verity felt the coldness of the sand on her bare feet when she discarded her flip-flops. Rylan threw off his towel. "C'mon, let's do this, babe," he said, laughing and moving them toward the water.

The evening light and the alcohol coerced to provide enough courage for Verity to fling off her towel, saying, "Tah-dah," and skip toward the sea and the incoming tide. Ankle-deep, shin-deep, then Rylan let go of Verity's hand and took the plunge.

"Woo-hoo," he shouted. "C'mon in; the water's fine," he laughed over the roar of the sea.

Verity knew the longer she stood there, the colder she would get, so she jumped in, catching the next high wave and riding it like a boat being bashed about in a rough sea. "Woo-hoo, that's cold; you lied," she admonished while readying herself for the next jump.

They laughed and played together like two kids in a bubble bath until, finally, Verity's feet found shallower ground, and she headed into shore while dodging outcrops of rock. "Brrrrrr, I'm getting out," she said over her shoulder.

Rylan was fast behind. They wrapped their towels around themselves. Verity emptied sand out of her flip-flops and shoved her feet into the gritty soles as they scurried toward the cabin.

"Cold shower?" shouted Rylan, laughing as he headed toward the outdoor shower.

"I thought you said it was warm."

"Uh-huh, that was around noon today; those pipes might be as cold as the ocean by now."

"No way I'm going in there,' Verity laughed. 'But you're welcome to join me in the civilized shower. My body's screaming for warmth right now."

"Yeah, I could use a bit of warmth myself, babe," Rylan replied, catching up with Verity on her way into the house.

The hot shower wrapped both of them in a warm fall of water as they soaped away the salt water and shampooed their hair. "You did it, Verity, your first swim in the nude. How's it feel?"

"This is how it feels," she replied, eyes wide and voice tender as she wrapped her arms around his broad shoulders and placed her lips on top of his. Rylan drew her in close, and they melted into each other as if nothing else in the world mattered at that moment other than the two of them.

Verity felt Rylan's hand run down her hips to her thigh. Rylan let the water pour over his face, then, filling his mouth with water, spurted it toward Verity. Instead of seeking revenge or just laughing it off, she stood still for a moment, gazing at Rylan, then placed her hands on the back of his head and pulled him close. They kissed under the cascade of water until Verity drew back and stepped out of the shower. She flew up the steps onto the verandah and hurried into the warmth of her bedroom.

While she dried off, Rylan grabbed his towel and stepped up to the verandah to retrieve his dry clothes. Instead of getting dressed, he watched from outside the screen door, shut against any possible invading insects, as Verity slipped into a sheer white negligee. She could feel Rylan's eyes on her as he slid open the screen, shut it behind him, and moved toward Verity, leaving his towel on the verandah floor.

"You're not going to need that," he whispered, moving closer to Verity. He caressed the bare skin of her arms, making it tingle with each stroke. He slid her spaghetti straps down her shoulders, and her negligee fell to her waist. She pushed it to the floor. Then, sweeping her hands up the back of Rylan's head, she moaned softly. He brushed her lips with his and firmly pulled her naked body in close.

By the time Rylan gently pulled away, Verity was left aching for his touch. Her lips hovered near his, drawn to him like a magnet. Her body burned for him. *How did I fall for him so fast?* The fire he'd ignited in her was one she didn't ever want to extinguish.

With daybreak streaming through the light curtains, Verity opened her eyes at sunrise. A delicious sense of fulfillment permeated her waking moments, her bedsheets still holding the scent of their lovemaking. *I want to see where he lives, sleep in his bed, sink into his very soul.*

She checked the clock at 6:45 a.m., sat up in bed, and just as she was thinking of getting up to see where Rylan was, he sailed into the room with a breakfast tray.

"Mornin', babe, how was your night?" Dimples, thick black hair, impossibly blue eyes. Before she could answer, Rylan said, "Shall we have this out on the verandah?"

"We shall; how lovely, thank you so much, Rylan...for everything." Verity smiled sweetly, rose from the bed, and slipped into a blue silk robe.

They enjoyed their morning coffee and the spicy-sweet flavour of cinnamon toast in Verity's favourite nook. "Hmm," said Verity, "the flavor of cinnamon reminds me of us."

"Huh?" said Rylan, pausing to consider her remark. "The spicy part, I get; no mystery there." He winked at her and squeezed her thigh, just above her knee, causing her to laugh.

"And sweet," she insisted. "Don't forget the huge component of sweet in there."

Rylan jumped on Verity's bandwagon. "Our lovemaking is so sensuously sweet that one of my love names for you from now on is going to be *Sweetness*. Because you are the epitome of sweet; the sweetest of the sweet." Rylan smiled, looking pleased with himself.

Verity brushed the back of her hand over Rylan's raspy morning stubble. "And that's because you fill me up with sugar," she smiled, placing her hands on both sides of his head and drawing his lips towards hers.

When Rylan said he had to leave for work, she felt the pain of his absence even before he left. *Please just stay here with me, maybe even forever.*

"What's on for you today, babe?" Rylan kickstarted his motor-cycle and, through the engine's noise, Verity said, "Absolutely nothing planned; that's a luxury of the highest order for me."

"Enjoy the luxury. Some of us have to work," Rylan quipped. He leaned in for a goodbye kiss, saying, "I've got your number. Let's talk soon." Before she could ask for his in return, he sped down the driveway and out onto the Queen's Highway.

Verity stood there for a moment, reflecting on her time spent with Rylan. *On only my sixth night here, I had a gorgeous man in my bed - not just gorgeous, but so much fun, and not someone just passing through, but a local with a steady job.*

She couldn't help herself because she was a strong visualizer. She imagined their wedding, their honeymoon, their children. She caught herself, her mind skidding to a halt. *Rick.* She couldn't forget him, even if she wanted to. But this... what she was feeling now— this connection with Rylan—it was different. And it felt like a betrayal. *Get a grip, Verity.*

As she headed back up the verandah steps, Verity started to gather the dishes from the night before and this morning. Then she stopped short, deciding to leave them there until she felt like cleaning them up. *This is the new me. No schedules to keep, no employers or colleagues or public to answer to, no husband, no friends.* She locked the doors, threw a cassette into the player, turned up the volume just shy of far-too-loud, and decided to have a bubble bath that might last all day if she felt like it.

She poured a bottle of tangerine-scented liquid into the water running full blast, lit half a dozen candles even though it was only 7:45 a.m., and set them around the deep bathtub. She pushed the small window wide open to help the steam escape and sank into mounds of foam. Leaning back against the headrest, thoughts of their evening swim, gazing at the stars in a full-moon sky intersected by branches of the casuarina trees, the exquisite feel of Rylan's bare skin next to hers, and the ecstasy of making love to a man that Verity imagined could be the man of her dreams, she was in a different world when, over the loud music, she heard heavy rhythmic pounding on her front door. The kind that normally can't be ignored.

Verity's former self might have hurried out of the bath, dried herself off, grabbed a bathrobe, and ran to the front door to take a peek out the curtain. She might have shouted out for some kind of identification if it was a stranger. Except for Rylan and the caretaker William, it surely would be a stranger.

As for the new Verity, she was having a bath. Languishing in a tub filled to the brim was not only a luxury she afforded herself today, June 24, which happened to be her 25th birthday, but Verity determined that from this day forward (at least while on vacation), she would do what she damn well pleased. *Does that mean I can't do what I damn well please when I'm back in Vancouver? Then why go back?*

The music filled the room, soft and melodic, the kind that made you sway even when you didn't mean to. She let the notes carry her deeper into the moment, into a place where the world couldn't reach her. The flickering candles cast dancing shadows on the walls as if the whole room was holding its breath, waiting for her to make a decision.

The pounding reverberated through the walls, but Verity barely flinched. It was as if the force of it couldn't touch her, couldn't pierce the bubble of serenity she'd wrapped herself in. She felt almost rebellious, a quiet defiance rising in her chest. *Let them wait.* Today was hers.

Ignoring the incessant pounding on the front door, Verity focused on the fragrant suds floating on top of the warm water surrounding her. When she sliced her hand through the mounds of white meringue, she imagined serving slices of pie to her imaginary friends. Today, Verity had only one friend in Exuma (unless she counted Gina), and she was certain that she would not be pounding on her door in this way, today of all days.

The heat of the water enveloped her like a second skin, a weightless embrace that promised nothing but the indulgence of now. For the first time in ages, she was truly alone—without the ticking of a clock, without obligations. This was her moment, and it felt like a reclamation of something she'd long forgotten.

CHAPTER 8

*M*onday, June 24

By lunchtime, Verity could feel the heat of the day building to the point that she felt like wearing nothing at all. Instead, she slipped on her lightest sundress without any under-wear, planted her wide-brimmed hat on top of her head, left her flip-flops at home, and headed out the door away from the large rocks to the right.

Verity knew she'd never have been able to take months off work to enjoy this island paradise. With the inheritance from her aunt, however, she could choose not to work ever again. But the truth was, given a choice, she wouldn't have traded her dear Aunt Lucy for all the money in the world. *You're in my heart, always.*

Daily sunshine gave Verity's skin a dark tan. Going without makeup now felt as natural to her as a new rosebud opening to the light, exposing its true beauty.

Walking along with her feet in the shallow water, Verity reached Gina's stone cottage and remembered the slamming door. She saw Gina, with her trademark long platinum blond hair, sitting at the side of the house. She was wearing a floral shift and smoking a cigarette.

"Hey there," she shouted, rising from her chair and walking across her front yard toward Verity. "Just a moment," she said, descending the stone steps and landing on the sandy beach.

Verity paused, wondering what "the most enigmatic" renter of Casuarina House had to say this morning.

"If you have a moment, why don't you join me?" Gina asked, sweeping her hand toward a couple of beach chairs sitting in her yard. Gina's cottage was nestled into the side of the hill, a little off the beaten path, surrounded by low bushes and vibrant, sun-bleached flowers. The stone steps led down to the sand, where her beach chairs sat like old friends waiting to be used. "And can I offer you an ice-cold brew?"

Woah, this woman is eager. It's almost like she was waiting for me.

"I'd love a glass of water, please, if you don't mind." Verity stepped up the low bank to Gina's front yard and sat down in one of the red beach chairs. Verity felt like enjoying her special day on her own, drinking in the pleasures of the island. Yet, she didn't want to be rude.

"I'll be there terreckly," Gina said, using local vernacular for *directly*, as she disappeared into her cottage. While Verity was still pondering this sudden turn of events, Gina emerged with a frosty bottle of beer in one hand and a glass of water on ice in the other.

She smirked, eyes twinkling. "Ah, nothing like an ice-cold beer on a hot summer day," she said, raising her bottle as if she were about to make a toast to something unspeakably important.

"Cheers,'"Verity replied, a little taken aback by Gina's flair

"And how're you liking Casuarina House, Verity?"

"Oh, you know where I am?"

"Yes, you'll find that everyone knows everyone else's business here. We even have a word for people who like to gossip; we say they like to 'tote news'.

"Hmm, well, I hope people aren't gossiping about me. I mean, what could they possibly know or guess? Really, I mostly just stay on this beach, so far anyway."

Gina looked amused. "I can tell you for certain that some are wondering what happened to me and Rylan." Gina seemed to stop in mid-stream and stare directly at Verity.

Verity almost choked on her water. "Wha'? You mean you and Rylan used to date?"

Gina laughed, but Verity thought it seemed affected. "Oh, yeah. Me 'n' Rylan were a couple, and he ended it not that long before you arrived here on the island."

Verity shifted uncomfortably in her chair, her mind racing. She couldn't help but imagine Gina and Rylan together. Her heart gave a little pang, but she forced the thought away, focusing on her cool glass of water instead. "Well, uh, gosh, Gina, I'm sorry to hear that. I, I don't know what to say."

"Say nothin', darlin'. It is what it is, I guess. I do so love that man, though; I'll make no secret of that."

"Yes." Verity struggled for words. "He's really quite special, isn't he?"

"Uh-huh. I'd honestly say that Rylan was my true love; I don't think I'll ever get over him, but never mind...." Gina took another swig of her beer. "None of it matters now, does it? I mean, if you two plan on sticking together?"

Verity felt the weight of Gina's words. The woman wasn't just talking about a past romance—she was still very much living in it, clinging to the ghost of something lost.

"Uh, what you two had was obviously special." Verity paused, trying to find the right words. "I want you to know that I knew nothing about this, Gina. That's all." Verity looked away, thinking about her exit.

"Oh, I know; not your fault. You wouldn't understand that anyone with my background has pretty low self-esteem. And for me to be dating a man who treated me with respect, again after the history I had with men, well, that did a lot for my self-esteem." She took another swig of beer. "I won't pull any punches here, hon. Rylan is someone I'd have died to hold on to."

And then it struck Verity. "Uh, was that you pounding on my front door this morning?"

"Huh?" Gina knitted her brow. "No, not me. Maybe you had a parcel delivery or something?"

"I didn't see anything, not that I checked for any parcel."

Verity cleared her throat, shifting gears. "By the way, Gina, how does one get mail around here?" It was a simple question, but in the context of their conversation, it helped her put some space between herself and the awkwardness of the moment.

"Oh, you'd have to buy a post office box from the post office in town."

Verity thought about her parents and about Rick. *It's about time I let them know how to contact me.* "You know, Gina, I'm going into town this afternoon, so I'll say goodbye for now, and thanks for your hospitality."

They both stood up. "Okay, sugar, don't be a stranger," Gina said as she gathered up the bottles, turned, and walked up her front steps.

I'll head in the other direction next time.

CHAPTER 9

Friday, June 28

After four days of walking the beach and unwinding at the cottage, Verity was ready for a change of scene.

Georgetown buzzed with activity on Friday afternoon. The straw market brimmed with shoppers, and the grocery store's parking lot was nearly full. Verity circled the lot before finding a space further away, near a small café and what looked like a hardware store. Up the street, near the bank, children's voices rang out. She spotted two boys darting between parked cars, laughing as they tried to hide from each other.

"Stop skylackin' around!" a young woman called out, emerging from a side road.

At that moment, an old pickup truck rattled down toward the bank. Verity's breath caught as one of the boys suddenly bolted into the street.

"Stop!" she shouted, throwing up a hand toward the driver as she lunged forward.

The boy froze. Tires screeched. The truck jerked to a stop just in time.

The driver leaned out the window, face flushed. "Where'd that damn kid come from? He wasn't even lookin' where he was goin'."

Verity pressed a hand to her chest, trying to steady her pounding heart. The near miss had left her shaken.

The young woman reached the boys, eyes blazing. She grabbed the arm of the one who'd run into the street. "Jeffrey, you cannot just run out like that! You scared that driver to death, and—" She trailed off as her gaze landed on Verity. Her expression shifted from anger to something else—relief, maybe. "Miss, I don't know what to say. If you hadn't been there..." She rubbed her left hand anxiously with her right.

Verity offered a reassuring smile. "I'm just glad I could help. No harm done." She turned to the boys, softening. "You're lucky you're so cute."

The tension eased as the boys grinned.

With a final nod, Verity crossed the road and headed into the grocery store, still feeling the aftershocks of what had almost happened.

BEFORE LEAVING TOWN, Verity decided to pop into a shop called Lacey J's, resisting the urge to visit Rylan at work.

She paused outside, drawn to the display of brightly painted metal fish. They were the same ones she'd seen in George's Café—modeled after real fish, their colours vivid and true to life, with carefully crafted fins and authentic proportions. Even tiny baby fish swam among them.

Inside, the shop overflowed with handcrafted treasures. Large sculptures of tropical fish adorned the walls, their colours almost glowing under the lights. Shelves brimmed with pottery—mugs, soap dishes, bowls, and plates. A section near the back held guidebooks, while a few racks displayed island-made clothing.

A young, slender woman in a light blue sundress patterned with seashells greeted her. "Welcome to Lacey J's."

"Oh, thank you—what a gorgeous shop! Are you the owner?"

"I am. Been here close to five years now." She smiled, nodding.

Verity wandered over to a display of coffee mugs. She picked one up, running her fingers over the smooth, light turquoise glaze. White fish outlines swam across the surface. "I love this design," she said, smiling. "And I love that it's big enough for almost two cups of coffee." She laughed, placing her thumb over the white clay imprint just above the handle. "I can already picture myself having my coffee at Casuarina House tomorrow morning."

The woman's expression flickered with recognition. "Casuarina House? You're staying there?"

"Yes—everyone seems to know that name." Verity chuckled before adding, "I noticed the metal fish in your window match the ones in George's Café."

The woman's smile softened. "Yes, the café owner and I are in sync."

"Oh?" Verity asked, curiosity stirring.

"Uh-huh." The woman's gaze drifted slightly, as if lost in a fond memory.

Verity hesitated. She didn't want to pry—and she certainly didn't want to seem jealous—so she decided to buy the mug and move on.

Is the whole island in love with Rylan?

WHEN THE COTTAGE phone rang at 8:00 Friday evening, Verity hoped it was Rylan. Before picking up the receiver, she took a deep breath, reminding herself to use a low, sultry tone. *Deep, sexy voice.*

"Hello." She aimed for *inviting, confident*—more statement than question.

"Verity, it's Rylan. How's Friday night at Casuarina House?"

"Quiet. Ridiculously quiet," Verity replied. "The wine is good, but it's hard to toast alone."

His soft laugh sent a shiver through her. If only she could pull him through the phone, straight into her cozy cottage, where tealights flickered in the dim light.

"Oh," he said, his voice teasing, "do I sense an invitation?"

"I'd love to see you, Rylan." *Why be shy? This is the new me, and I'm liking me... so far, anyway.*

"You know I'd love nothing more than to spend the evening with you," he said, "but I'm otherwise committed. That said, I have an idea you might like."

"I'm listening."

"If you're up for an adventure, I'd love to take you somewhere special tomorrow. But I want it to be a surprise. Sound good?"

"I love surprises. Should I bring my bathing suit?"

"Oh. Thanks for thinking of that—although here in Exuma, you don't always need one."

She laughed. "You're kidding, right?"

"Maybe. Depends." His voice dipped suggestively. "We can test that theory sometime. But for tomorrow, I'll pick you up at ten. I'll pack lunch, and we'll make a day of it."

<u>Saturday</u>, June 29

The road to Cocoplum Beach was full of potholes and, without a sign to show people where to turn, few tourists ever visited that beach, explained Rylan. The motorcycle proceeded slowly, avoiding potholes, mud puddles, and thorny branches along the narrow, windy road to the beach. Rylan parked his motorcycle close to a broken-down shack littered with empty beer bottles and cigarette stubs.

Verity was silent, rendered breathless by the scene before her. The turquoise colour of the sea was the most perfect turquoise she'd ever seen. The shallow water was intersected with crescent-shaped, pristine white sandbars seemingly untarnished by human foot-prints. Not another person in sight. No structures were visible up and down the beach other than the broken-down shack at the entrance.

Verity turned to Rylan, her eyes wide with wonder. "People commonly describe such scenes as 'looking like a postcard,' and I guess that's because there just are no words to describe such perfec-tion. I mean, the sea is calm and clear, there's not a cloud in the sky, the temperature is warm. The only word I can think of to describe this place is *heaven*."

Rylan gave her a quick kiss on the lips. "I knew you'd like it here, sweetness. Let's find a spot to park our stuff and see if we can find some sand dollars."

"Ha, d'you think?"

"I guess I didn't tell you. The beach is known locally as Sand Dollar Beach, and for good reason."

Rylan brushed his hands over Verity's bare shoulders, making her feel feminine and sexy. Excited to look for sand dollars, she slipped away, gliding ahead of Rylan toward the nearest sandbar. Her filmy white dress was as light as the gossamer wings of a butterfly and, as she turned to look back at Rylan, she saw him standing perfectly still, his eyes fixed on her as she walked barefoot in the sand.

Verity drew her dress up over her head, revealing a coral-coloured bikini. She stuffed it into her bag and set it high up on the shore. As they stepped into the warm water, Verity kept looking up and down the beach, still amazed that they had it all to themselves.

She was barely shin-deep in water when she spotted a six-keyhole sand dollar lying in the sand. It was the first she'd seen in Exuma since her arrival. "Look, I found one," she pointed it out to Rylan, then stooped down to have a close look at it in its natural habitat. She admired the design with its six openings all around the circumference and what looked like an embossed flower design in the center.

Rylan was so enjoying Verity's delight in her find, that he forgot to warn her.

When Verity picked up the perfectly formed sand dollar, it crumbled like powder in her hands. "Oh, no," she said in dismay, "I broke it."

Rylan laughed. "Ver, I forgot to tell you just how fragile sand dollars are. And, if you're lucky enough to bring some home still intact when they dry out they are extremely brittle." Rylan took a few steps forward and found another. "Here, let me show you how I scoop them up." He used his hand to dig down into the sand under the shell so that the sand acted as a cushion to protect it.

"For you, my love," he said, bowing to Verity as he held out the pristine treasure and safely transferred it to Verity's hand. "One more thing you should know. If you come upon a sand dollar that is black or looks dirty, that one's still alive, so we need to leave those alone."

*Ah, I **knew** he was a kindred spirit.*

They walked the sandbars gathering sunray venuses, Cowrie helmets, Scotch bonnets, chestnut turbans, and lots of shells that Verity planned to look up in her reference book when she got home. There were lots of sunray venuses with both pink and yellow highlights but, when Verity spotted what looked like an angel's wing up ahead in the sand, she just stared at it for a moment, afraid it might break if she picked it up. But she wasn't about to leave it behind.

She carefully lifted the delicate pink shell from the sand and found that it was quite strong. The fan-shaped shell ended in a sturdy point, and Verity was lucky enough to find a double.

"Rylan, come see this," she shouted excitedly across the width of the sandbar. Finding a cluster of baby starfish, she reached down into the water, which was only still halfway up her calf, to pick one up. Turning it over, she could see the tentacles waving back and forth, so she put it back in the water.

"Yeah, there's just something about starfish, isn't there, babe?"

They carried their things to the far end of the beach, where they could see a cove that might be worth exploring. Since the tide was coming in, they had to step over the limbs of a fallen tree that weren't visible when they first arrived.

They sat on a huge log in the cove and ate their lunch. Rylan's spiked lemonade was still cold in the insulated pack. "I couldn't have imagined a more perfect day, babe. Thanks so much for bringing me here." Verity kissed his lips and said, "Let's wade out to that little island." She pointed to a small piece of land with some openings among the bushes.

"Oh, it's too far, I think, babe, especially with the tide coming in."

Verity kept looking at it, trying to judge the distance. When Rylan walked through water deep enough for swimming, he moved closer to an old wrecked boat half sunken in the inlet. Verity walked slowly toward the island and, the farther she got, the more convinced she became that she could easily swim the distance when the water got too deep to walk.

She heard the sound of an engine to her left and glanced to see a small motorboat coming near, driven by a woman in a white cap and red bathing suit. She shouted something that Verity couldn't hear, and Verity could see Rylan swimming toward the boat.

Ah, I knew it was too good to be true that we'd be together alone on Cocoplum for the entire day. As Verity continued walking, she laughed at herself for being annoyed that one other person showed up. *Major intrusion, ha!*

Soon, Verity became aware that the water was rising faster than she thought it would. By now she could feel it lapping against her armpits, and that's when her fear took hold. She tried to push images of her childhood near-drowning out of her head – her body submerged, bubbles rising to the surface, her arms flailing as she rose up to the surface but somehow unable to cry out for help.

Instead, Verity tried to concentrate on returning to safety. She turned around to face the shore but was alarmed speechless when her feet no longer touched the ground. She was afraid to scream in case she upset the delicate balance between staying afloat and going under. Besides, she felt foolish.

She saw Rylan and the woman laughing, oblivious to her plight. When the incoming tide came faster, she began to panic. Never a strong swimmer, she struggled to make progress, and it seemed to her that she was sliding out to sea rather than into shore. She began to feel helpless as terrifying images of submerging menaced her mind. She saw the bubbles, her flailing arms, her rising and falling without time to shout for help.

When she felt Rylan's strong arm reaching, slipping off, and then finally sweeping her forward to the safety of the motorboat, she was beyond relieved and grateful. And she was embarrassed.

"Are you okay?" Rylan wrapped his arms around her in the small boat, helping her calm down and trying to warm her. The female boater moved them close to the entranceway to the beach. They disembarked, thanked the boater, and walked toward the shack.

As they walked back to the motorcycle, Verity released some pent-up emotions. "I couldn't call for help," she cried, "I imagined my mouth filling with water." She shuddered to think of how much trouble she was in. "And I couldn't get your attention because you were talking to that woman."

Now Verity realized why she felt upset.

"I'm sorry, babe. I didn't realize you were trying to reach the island. I mean..."

"I know," Verity said, hanging her head, "I should've listened to you."

"And, as for the woman," Rylan said, "she asked for the name of the beach. Said she'd never seen such a beautiful place and wanted to make sure she could find it again."

Verity didn't reply. *Or maybe she spotted your impossibly blue eyes from 100 feet away.*

CHAPTER 10

Saturday, June 29 – Saturday, July 6

Back at Casuarina House, they showered off the salt water—Rylan in the outdoor shower, Verity inside. Verity made a quick stir-fry of shrimp and vegetables, and they rounded out the night with a glass of wine.

"I'm pretty bushed," Rylan said to Verity, who nodded her head in agreement. "I'll say goodnight here on the verandah. You don't need to walk me to my bike." Rylan drew Verity in tight and whispered in her ear. "You're my treasure, Ver, and I don't ever want to lose you. Please take care of yourself." He closed his eyes and kissed Verity passionately, leaving her a bit stunned. *How did our relationship elevate to this level already?*

DURING THE NEXT WEEK, Verity browsed the paperback books on the cottage bookshelf. Among them were a history of salt mining on the island, a picture book of Bahamian seashells, and a tourist guide to Nassau.

On Saturday morning, Rylan and Verity sat on the verandah, waiting. It was July 6, and the party boat was due any minute. Rylan wore a short-sleeved shirt unbuttoned all the way, revealing a leather string necklace with a black heart pendant. The shadow of stubble on his jaw gave him a rugged look that made Verity want to crawl onto his lap and forget about the boat altogether.

She had dressed for the occasion—a bright pink bikini under beige cotton shorts and a sleeveless white top. She was prepared for sun and swimming; the rest was a mystery, but apprehension niggled at her.

"Um," she started, "I ran into Gina again last Sunday." She waited. Nothing from Rylan.

"Yeah, and—it almost felt like she was waiting for me." Still nothing.

"So," she pressed, "you and Gina were lovers just before I came along?"

Rylan let out a groaning laugh. "I wouldn't put it that way, but I've heard she's the star of her own movie—the one where I jilted her."

"Jilted when I showed up?"

"Jilted whenever anyone showed up," he corrected. "Look, we dated for maybe three weeks when she first moved here. Then I realized she was a drug addict."

Verity blinked, absorbing that. "What kind of drugs?"

"Cocaine, for sure. Probably more. That's why she barely leaves her cottage." He exhaled. "And trust me, if she thinks I have even the thinnest attraction to her, she's hallucinating."

Verity exhaled, relieved. "Good to know. She made it sound like I was the reason for the breakup."

"Gina has money," she continued. "Where does she even get the stuff?"

"No idea. But you'll see things on the party boat," Rylan said. "I keep my nose—pardon the pun—out of it. I like my life too much to ruin it."

Verity's heart warmed at that. He was worth fighting for.

"There's The Seaglass," Rylan said, spotting the catamaran through his binoculars.

She grabbed her beach bag while he lifted his cooler, and they headed for the shore. The gleaming seventy-five-foot catamaran, topped with a turquoise sunshade, teemed with partygoers hanging over the sides, drinks in the air.

To the left, two women approached. Gina's long platinum hair was unmistakable, although a sequined mask hid her face. Her flamboyant dress and loud voice didn't match the image of a recluse. The woman beside her was unfamiliar.

"Hey, Gina, glad you could make it," Rylan said with a nod. *Ever the friendly business owner,* Verity mused. Gina's neon-orange bikini was barely concealed by a sheer cover-up.

"And hey, Jacks, have you met Verity?"

Jacks shook Verity's hand, her petite frame and cropped hair giving off a no-nonsense vibe—except for the thong and braless halter top.

The music swelled as the cat neared. A tall man in navy athletic shorts hollered, "Hey-ho!"

"Michael, my man!" Rylan called. "Can you grab the cooler?"

As the boat drifted close, Michael extended a ladder. Rylan handed up the cooler and then helped the women aboard.

The musky scent of marijuana hit Verity instantly, but as the boat picked up speed offshore, the breeze diluted it. She noted the life jackets and snorkeling gear—*at least some responsible choices were made here.*

Drinks flowed freely. Rylan passed her an ice-cold rum punch from his cooler. He lifted his gin on the rocks in a toast, then grinned at her, swaying to the music.

Most of the men had shoulder-length hair, some with handlebar mustaches—so different from Rylan's clean-cut look.

Verity scanned the crowd. A dark-haired woman in a sheer dress danced wildly, arms high. Nearby, another woman's orange top barely qualified as clothing. Everywhere, women in neon bikinis and thongs flaunted bronzed skin, their hips rolling to the beat. Verity resisted the urge to stare.

Cassie and Janesta approached Rylan, all too eager.

"Hey, you two," Rylan said. "Meet my girlfriend."

The word sent a thrill through Verity. Had he sensed her jealousy? Or was he claiming her here, now?

"I see you already know my boyfriend," she teased, offering her name.

Cassie and Janesta's enthusiasm dimmed as they moved on.

Far out at sea, the cat dropped anchor. Snorkelers jumped in despite the choppy water.

"I don't know, Rylan. Think it's safe?" Verity asked, gripping his arm.

"I'll let you know, babe." Mask and snorkel in place, he descended the ladder.

Verity watched him swim farther out, his head lifting now and then to check his surroundings. Gina's platinum hair soon bobbed beside him. They paused together, observing something below the surface. *A sea turtle? A stingray?*

Then Verity saw it—Gina slipping her hand into Rylan's.

Heat flushed her cheeks. Without a second thought, she stripped to her bikini, grabbed a mask and snorkel, and headed for the ladder.

The water was a shock against her skin. She gripped the mouthpiece and sealed her lips around it.

Relax. You're okay.

Memories of a childhood near-drowning surfaced, but she pushed them back, visualizing herself breathing steadily, floating safely.

She lifted her head to find Rylan. At least five others snorkeled nearby—if anything went wrong, she could grab one of them.

She swam forward, determined.

CHAPTER 11

Verity awoke on Sunday morning without Rylan beside her. She glanced at her bedside clock and saw that she'd slept in later than usual. Feeling a bit woozy, Verity slipped out from under the covers and, before heading to the kitchen, she peeked out the sliding glass door. She spotted Rylan sauntering along the rolling grounds to the left of the cottage.

Verity carried her water glass out the front door and met up with Rylan. "Hey, good morning. I hope you're feeling a bit perkier than I am."

"Probably too much gin last night," Rylan replied, "but at least I stay away from the harder stuff—no toking up or sniffing white lines for me."

"Ah, so that's what they were doing down there on the lower deck." Verity shrugged her right shoulder. "I don't know much about the drug scene," she said, matter-of-factly.

"No, hopefully, it's not big with those in the teaching profession," Rylan laughed. "As you know, weed and cocaine are both illegal here in the Bahamas, so what happens on the party boat is top secret." He looked straight at Verity to help make his point.

"Honestly, yesterday felt like a brush with the criminal under-world. And, while it was intriguing and fun to glimpse the wild side of life, I won't be adding the party boat scene to my repertoire."

"Understood completely, babe. I feel the same way. When I do go, which is rare, I keep my nose clean."

"Guilty by association, Rylan," Verity teased. "Want me to make us some breakfast?" she asked, putting her arm around his waist.

"You know, I'm going to take a rain check on that, sweetness. I have to get myself sorted out for work tomorrow, so I'm going to hit the road now."

Their lips drew each other like magnets as they embraced for a time that never seemed long enough these days. They held each other under the casuarinas, their hands tracing familiar paths, the sweetness of the moment enough to carry them through until next time.

It was Monday morning, and Verity felt great. She hopped out of bed, enjoying her usual lazy breakfast, before heading straight to the beach. Her curiosity about Jacks' property had been piqued ever since their encounter on the boat. Despite having passed it many times, she hadn't given it much thought until she met Jacks.

Set back from the shore, the cottage looked like a rectangular block with a flat roof—a stark contrast to the lush surroundings. *Utility shed,* was Verity's first impression. The square building was painted gray stucco, giving it a concrete-block vibe, and its rust-coloured roof seemed out of place. The only window facing the ocean seemed like an afterthought, adding to the utilitarian feel. The surrounding land was a scruffy mix of grass and sand, giving the whole place an unkempt air.

To get a better look, Verity climbed the bank, shading her eyes from the sun as she peered into the distance. That's when she heard Jacks' voice behind her. "Hey, I know you," she said with a laugh, touching Verity's arm and making her jump.

"Holy man, you scared me to death! Where'd you come from?"

Jacks burst into laughter. "I spent the night at Gina's but figured it was time to get my butt in gear and head back home."

By now, Verity had recovered but still felt a bit embarrassed. *Caught snooping.* "Forgive me, but after meeting you on the boat, I was curious to see your place."

"No worries," Jacks chuckled. "Here, let me show you so you don't have to sneak around like a cat burglar." She slid her arm around Verity's shoulders, pulling her in close. "But I did enjoy the sight of you trying to get a better view," she teased.

Jacks unlocked the front door and swept it open, revealing a surprising contrast inside. The furnishings were striking. The red leather loveseat and matching chairs looked welcoming, and a red brick fireplace made the space feel homely. The British India wool carpet added a touch of luxury, while the floor-to-ceiling bookcases on either side of the fireplace gave the place an executive vibe—completely at odds with the exterior.

Verity studied the bookshelves, noticing titles by Hemingway, Nietzsche, and Sartre. "Oh, classy, Jacks. I wasn't expecting this after seeing the outside."

"Not my style, I know," Jacks laughed. "It's comfortable enough for now, though. If I ever decide to tear it down and build something bigger, well, I've got the option."

Verity could hardly imagine having such options. "So you just park here and visit friends, and then what—fly off to your other properties?"

"Ha, yeah, something like that," Jacks said with a grin. "Come on, I'll show you something." She led Verity around the back of the building.

Verity gasped when she saw a small airplane resting on a grass runway, with a fuel tank nearby. "You...you have your own plane?" she asked, incredulous.

"Uh-huh," Jacks said, sounding smug but proud. "I'm guessing you don't know many female pilots?"

"Ah, no, can't say that I do." Verity laughed. "I mean, well, until now. Do you actually own this plane, Jacks?"

"Yep. Pretty cool, right?"

Verity paused for a moment before teasing, "So, you're either a millionaire, a billionaire... or you fly goods, or maybe you're a flying doctor. I give up. Please, enlighten me."

Jacks laughed—without sound—but Verity could see her abs shake as she suppressed it. "You're right. My dad's a multi-millionaire, and I inherited a pretty nice trust from my grandfather. Gives me the freedom to do what I want, mostly."

Verity was taken aback. "Wow, Jacks, that's... I can't even imagine that kind of life."

"Well, I can give you a glimpse if you want," Jacks said with a suggestive raise of her eyebrows.

"Yeah, I guess... What do you mean, exactly?"

"You might enjoy flying over to Nassau sometime. A lot of famous people live on Paradise Island. I party there all the time."

Verity's instinctive caution flared. "Famous, paradise, party..." She shifted on her feet, one hand on her hip. "I'm not sure, Jacks. What's the deal?"

Jacks grinned. "I can pick you up next Friday. We can stay in Nassau for the weekend, and I'll fly you back on Sunday. Sound good?"

Verity hesitated, thoughts swirling. "Okay, I guess... What should I bring?"

Jacks shrugged. "Maybe something fancy for Saturday night. But, hey, a lot of my friends have an 'anything goes' attitude. So really, you can't go wrong. But you seem like you'd want to follow some sort of protocol, right? Don't worry, I'll make sure you're comfortable."

"Thanks, Jacks. I appreciate it. And I'm sure you realize I'm not into illicit drugs," Verity blurted out, realizing how it must sound. "But, uh... my curiosity does tend to push me toward places I might not normally go."

"I get it," Jacks said, her tone light. "It's a mixed bag. You'll probably find some people like you there, too."

"Got it. Okay, I'll be ready Friday at... what time?"

"We'll leave at seven sharp. It's only a forty-minute flight to Nassau, so be here by a quarter to, and we're good. I'll stay at the Emerald Beach Hotel Friday night, then hire a limo to take us to Paradise Island on Saturday. Sound good?"

Verity spent the next three days thinking about what to pack, wondering if she should buy any makeup. After months of not wearing any, it felt like a strange novelty.

CHAPTER 12

Friday, July 12 – Sunday, July 14

By the time Jacks and Verity settled into their luxury hotel suite in Nassau, they had time for a relaxing dinner followed by a dessert cocktail in the lounge. Verity appreciated the extra touches–the gold-rimmed, gold-stemmed cocktail glass that held her rich, green-hued dessert drink. She savoured each sip of her minty chocolate Grasshopper, content that it was the perfect end to her meal of Roasted Bahamian Lobster Tail on the Shell.

DRIVING across the bridge connecting the island of New Providence to Paradise Island, the limo driver advised that the bridge was built eight years ago as part of efforts to enhance tourism in the Bahamas. Verity barely listened, shifting to her left in the plush leather backseat, trying to take in the views ahead of the luxury hotel where they would spend Saturday night.

Paradise Island Hotel stretched out like the wings of a maple tree seed pod, with villas neatly aligned on the far side of the pool. Palm trees swayed gently in the morning breeze as vacationers lounged by the pool or headed toward the endless beach. The whiteness of the resort buildings complemented the white sand and highlighted the turquoise waters.

Jacks had booked a penthouse suite facing the ocean.

"Oh, I like your style, Jacks," Verity said, throwing open the draperies and gazing down at the stunning view.

"Yeah, I know. I love this place. Want to go snorkeling? Or scuba diving? How 'bout tennis or golf? There's even horseback riding if you're into that."

Verity began unpacking her belongings, considering the options.

"Or, if you'd rather," Jacks continued, "we can just take a long walk on the beach, maybe go swimming, or have a few drinks by the pool."

"It all sounds good, Jacks, honestly. What time's the party tonight?"

"Starts at six. They've rented the entire dining room, so we can have dinner there and carry on into the evening."

"Whoa! Who are *they*, Jacks? Obviously, people I need to get to know," Verity laughed.

She slipped out of her off-the-shoulder cocktail dress and hung it in the closet, using the ribbons attached to the dress to keep it in place. "Do you think this dress will cut it in these swanky surroundings?" she asked, glancing over at Jacks.

Verity had packed only one dress she thought might work for the occasion. Living in Exuma, she knew that shopping for party clothes was practically out of the question.

"I bet that'll look gorgeous on you, Verity." Jacks smiled. "And I like those sparkly stilettos. I'm wearing this." She lifted a powder blue silk slip dress and champagne-coloured heels. "Cool and comfy," she added, pleased with her choice.

∼

THEY'D AGREED that seventy-nine degrees was too hot to play tennis, so they opted for an afternoon of private scuba lessons followed by lunch.

At the bottom of the sea, the murky water obscured the clear view Verity had enjoyed the last time she snorkeled. She and Jacks stayed close to one another, pointing out zebrafish, squirrelfish, and one of Verity's favourites: parrotfish. Their teeth formed a parrot's beak, a distinguishing feature. Verity's body shook with excitement as she stretched her arm out and pointed sharply, hoping Jacks wouldn't miss it. This parrotfish was the most beautiful she'd seen so far, its opalescent blues mixed with green, orange, and yellow near its mouth, *almost like the strokes of an artist's brush,* Verity mused. The instructor pointed out a green moray eel tucked into a rocky crevice, prompting Verity and Jacks to swim farther away—much farther.

As time passed, Verity kept a careful eye on her air tank. This time, the level had dropped to a worrisome point. She tapped Jacks on the arm, pointing to her air level indicator. Jacks shrugged, and the two of them scanned the surroundings, looking for the instructor, but he was nowhere to be found.

Feeling the weight of her tank and the pressure of her mask and snorkel tube, Verity panicked and started swimming toward the surface. Jacks followed, and when they both broke the surface, Verity was still frantic, struggling to shed the heavy tank. Disoriented, her eyes scanned to the right. People were standing on the shore, not far away. She felt a wave of relief, although she felt foolish. She and Jacks had been within walking distance of shore the whole time.

Soon, the errant instructor surfaced, and they all swam back to land.

THE SHEER ENJOYMENT of the extravagant lunch paid for by Jacks quickly pushed any embarrassment out of Verity's mind. They chatted and laughed the afternoon away, their connection growing hour by hour.

When Verity felt the time was right, she asked, "So, do you mind if I ask you a nosy question, Jacks?"

Verity thought she saw a slight stiffening in Jacks when she grew quiet.

"Fire away," she said, her tone trying to sound casual and confident, but Verity detected a slight undercurrent of uncertainty. Jacks listened intently.

"So, when I noticed your dental diamond on the party boat, you said something about not wanting a diamond on your finger...may I ask what that's about?"

Jacks laughed, sounding somewhat relieved, though Verity wasn't sure if that was just her imagination. *I think most people freeze when someone asks, 'Do you mind if I ask you a question?'*

"I don't mind at all," Jacks said. "Believe it or not, I was married for a short while to someone who, I later found out, married me only for my money."

"Oh, I'm sorry to hear that, Jacks. How heartbreaking that must have been."

"Heartbreaking is one word; infuriating, devastating, and astounding are others." Jacks lifted her cocktail glass to her lips and glanced out to sea.

"How did you find out the truth?"

"I overheard a conversation between my husband and one of his friends. He blatantly admitted he'd married me for my money and that my family fortune would be his one day." Jacks smirked, shaking her head at the memory.

"Wow. I mean, wow. I can't imagine the shock, the pain. I bet you were in divorce court faster than a jaguar runs a mile."

Jacks nodded. "Oh, you can be sure that once Daddy caught wind of the plan, it was all over in a few days. He was out on his ass, flung back into the poverty he so deserved."

"Okay, now I understand why no wedding rings for you," Verity said, smiling and raising her glass in a toast to Jacks. "It's amazing how devious we humans can be when the motivation is strong enough."

"Yeah, there can be strong motivations, but we don't all act on them," Jacks replied.

They were quiet for a moment, lost in their thoughts. Then Verity spoke again.

"There were plenty of clues that my Charlie was having an affair, in retrospect. At the time, I guess I just chose not to notice. But the classic lipstick on the collar was a tip-off I couldn't ignore, and then I finally let myself put two and two together."

Jacks nodded, her lips curling downward. "Yes, and it's amazing how we turn a blind eye to things right under our noses."

"True," Verity said, "but we're both much more aware now, right?" They shared a laugh before their parfaits were served, quickly melting in the hot afternoon sun.

Popping a red cherry into her mouth, Jacks asked, "And how's it going with Rylan?" Her eyes brightened as she waited for Verity's answer.

Verity's beaming smile said it all. "You know, from the minute I laid eyes on that gorgeous man, I fast-forwarded to our honeymoon." She laughed at her boldness, and Jacks tilted her head back in her chair, laughing toward the sky.

"And every time he looks at me, I feel like we're the only two people in the world. Every time he touches me, I'm transported to another universe."

Relaxed by the alcohol and the warm sun seeping through her thin dress—something that always made her feel sexy—Verity continued, while Jacks seemed mesmerized by her flow of words.

"I was drawn to Rylan like I've never been drawn to any other man, not even my ex. I loved the sound of his voice, the way his deep blue eyes complemented his thick black hair. His confidence. His charisma." Verity quickly added, "But he's not one of those charismatic people who always seem to have an agenda."

"What do you mean?"

"With Rylan, everything just seemed natural. I never felt like he was trying to charm me to take advantage. Sure, I admit I was jealous of other women around him—something I'd never felt before. I never thought of myself as the jealous type, but with him..." Verity's voice trailed off, a slight smile on her lips.

Jacks narrowed her eyes, thinking. "Hmm, do you think your jealousy was sending you a message?"

Verity nodded. "Yes, I think it was letting me know that Rylan's really something special, and I need to fight to keep him—especially here in Exuma, where the demand for male attention far exceeds the supply," she chuckled.

"From what I know with the limited time I've spent in Exuma, Rylan's definitely the prize of the island as far as women are concerned," Jacks added.

"Yes, I can see that, but you know what?" Verity paused, gauging Jacks' reaction. "He knows it too, but he doesn't flaunt it. And I've never known him to be anything but respectful toward women."

"Sounds like you've got a real treasure there, Ver. Good on ya."

Their conversation felt effortless. Time zipped by, and soon Party Time arrived. Before they left their hotel room, dressed and ready for the event, Jacks laughed briefly and said, "Oh, by the way, you're welcome to come onto my property anytime. No need to stand on the breakwater and gawk in." They shared a laugh, and Verity appreciated the offer but couldn't imagine walking around Jacks' property for any reason.

As they entered the open-air bar and lounge at 6 pm, Verity tried not to stare at a couple who looked like Mick and Bianca Jagger. 'Bianca' wore a show-stopping outfit with red sequins—everything red: beret, jacket slung over her shoulders, full skirt of her floor-length halter-top dress. Her companion wore a white shirt with a pointed collar, at least four buttons undone, and a navy pinstriped suit. Swanky.

Jacks seemed to be having fun watching Verity enjoy herself. "Oh, how very au courant," Jacks said, referring to the red sequined outfit. They raised their brows in unison. Jacks easily engaged in conversation with everyone she knew—and even those she didn't. People often asked about her father.

When a server offered a glass of champagne, they obligingly took one and strolled across the room to admire the view outside. People lounging in chairs looked back at them, probably curious about the parade of glamour assembling in the dining area.

"Evening, Jacks," said a woman wearing bright red lipstick. *How does she not get it on her teeth?* A giant white flower pin contrasted her black, one-shoulder mini-dress. She wore slouchy gold boots and held her champagne flute elegantly in a gloved hand.

"Meredith, I was hoping you'd be here. Where's Anthony?"

"Ah, he's late getting back from Goat Cay, darlin'. He'll be along." Meredith didn't seem to notice Verity even though she was standing just a foot away. Instead, she scanned the room while talking to Jacks. "Ah, there's Shandy," she said and walked off.

"Hmm, interesting manners," Verity muttered to Jacks.

Jacks chuckled. "Yeah, some of the ultra-rich think they're above what the rest of us consider common courtesies."

"I could sit here and people-watch all night," Verity said, just as a tall woman with long, thick black hair entered the room in a barely-there dress, leaving almost nothing to the imagination. Her companion smiled with pride as they entered the crowd of partygoers, stopping now and then to chat.

When the band started playing *Keep on Movin'* by Bob Marley and the Wailers, people flocked to the dance floor like ants to honey. "Perfect song for smokin' a joint," someone said from the sidelines. Verity laughed to herself when she heard the lyrics, "Lord, I gotta keep on movin' where I can't be found." *Hey, are they talkin' 'bout me?*

As the reggae tunes continued, the lead singer got more and more energetic, dancing across the stage like a steel marble on a pinball machine. "What's he on?" Jacks laughed. She and Verity moved across the dance floor, their hips in sync with the bass guitar's repeated rhythm. The combination of reggae and alcohol lulled Verity into a quiet peace, the same kind of tranquility she felt with Rylan. *But wait, I used to feel that way with Rick, too.*

At nine o'clock, two servers carried in a huge cake shaped like a harmonica, covered in lit candles. The band started playing *Happy Birthday*, and the room erupted into song and laughter. Verity smiled as the cake was placed in front of the island's owner. *I guess he plays harmonica.*

Grooving to the music and sipping Yellow Bird cocktails, Verity found that the hours slipped by quickly. Jacks pointed out and introduced her to various celebrities from entertainment, sports, politics, fashion, modelling, and even royalty.

When she was introduced to the owner of Paradise Island, a supermarket heir, Verity blurted out, "Ha, my first job was as a grocery store cashier." That's all she could think of saying. When there was no response, she shrank away from the conversation and headed outside by the pool. *I've got nothing in common with these people.*

"C'mon in," a soft, velvety male voice called from a far corner of the pool, raising his glass high. *Is he from the party? Is he even wearing clothes?*

Verity smiled politely and decided to head back through the lobby. She needed a change of scene and to escape the stench of cigar smoke from a group of men lounging on lawn chairs. As she passed through, she overheard a woman dripping in jewels admonishing the concierge.

"But I told you I wanted the homemade dog treats! These are synthetic—anyone can see that. Bentley will be utterly insulted."

Stepping into the lounge, Verity spotted Jacks, on fire, dancing with everyone within reach. At exactly midnight, a crackling sound echoed across the water as a grand display of fireworks lit up the sky. People rushed to the balcony, drinks in hand, still moving to the rhythms of reggae.

Verity scanned the bar, feeling a light touch on her arm. She turned to see a deeply tanned man with curly blonde hair, dressed in denim shorts and an open shirt.

"You look like you're searching for someone," he said, a grin in his eyes.

Verity let out a light laugh. "Ah, no—I think he's just not here."

Shrugging off her pre-party jitters, she embraced the carefree vibe.

"What say we hit the beach?" she asked.

The stranger raised an eyebrow. "You better ditch those stilettos first."

With a sweep of his hand, he gestured to a nearby chair. "Sit down, Cinderella, and we'll get those shoes off before the coach turns into a pumpkin."

"And can I interest you in some port?" he added, winking.

"Oh, sounds lovely," Verity said, recalling a port she'd enjoyed last Christmas in Whistler with Rick—blissfully snowed in, sharing wine by the fire.

"You'll have to visit my yacht to taste it," he said with a grin. "But I promise, it'll be worth every sip."

"How's that?" Verity raised an eyebrow. "Is it some special kind of port?"

"Does 1827 Villar D'Allan mean anything to you?"

Verity wasn't sure whether to be impressed or insulted, but she decided to play along.

"Oh, vintage port, very special," she said, her tone playful. "No matter how rummy your yacht is, I'm sure it's worth it." She questioned her own sobriety.

"In that case," he said, extending his hand, "I'm Apollo. And you are...?"

"Selene," she said, pleased with her quick thinking. "It means moon."

"Ah, appropriate," he said with a smile. "*Selini* means moon, you know."

"I know," Verity lied. "And I know the moon is lit by the sun." She tilted her head playfully. "So I assume the blond hair is intentional?"

Apollo's laugh was deep, and he seemed to enjoy the exchange. "Indeed, Apollo is the god of the sun. But you probably knew that already."

They both laughed at their cleverness, and Apollo—*Was that really his name?*—took her hand as they stood.

"May I?" he asked, taking her stilettos and leading her out.

Outside, thousands of tiny white lights twinkled around hedges. The air was warm, the music sweet, and the fragrance of yellow elder flowers hung in the air. Verity's thoughts drifted to Rylan, and a tinge of guilt crept in when she realized she hadn't thought of Rick first.

Apollo's yacht, once owned by a sheik, was a masterpiece—a movie theatre, a helicopter pad, and a hot tub as big as a pond.

Verity tried not to look impressed. "It's beautiful," she said, raising her crystal glass. "You're a lucky man." Their glasses clinked as they exchanged a lingering gaze.

The port's intense sweetness coated her mouth, reminding her of molasses. "This is exquisite," she said, savouring the aftertaste. "Happiness in a glass, I'd say."

"I agree," Apollo said, smiling as he gently kissed her neck. "It's a pleasure to see you happy."

Verity tried to push back the question—*Was it reckless to sip this rare, celebratory port with a stranger? Exciting? A mistake? Maybe.* But one thing she knew for sure—she didn't care what anyone else thought. Before she could dwell on it, Apollo's voice cut through her musings.

"Life is a celebration, is it not?" he said, taking the empty glass from her hand. "Care to join me in the hot tub, my dear?"

Normally, the phrase *my dear* would have irritated her, but tonight she simply nodded and began to undress. Why not? No commitments. No expectations.

Rylan briefly crossed her mind, but she pushed the thought away before it could settle.

In the hot tub, the warmth made her sleepy, the soft music in the background lulling her. Apollo's voice drifted in and out.

He climbed out, wrapping a thick white towel around his waist, then held out another—large, plush, and warmed from the towel heater. She stepped into it gratefully, sighing as the comforting heat chased away the lingering chill of the night.

"You can freshen up in here," he said, nodding toward a bathroom with gold fixtures. "There's a bathrobe, too, if you like."

Verity entered the bathroom, wiping away the smudged makeup. She barely had the energy to stay upright. The gold-topped crystal bottle on the vanity released the sweet scent of jasmine, a final reminder of her brush with the ultra-rich.

When she opened the bathroom door, Apollo walked toward her in a silk robe.

"Oh, you got dressed," he said, a hint of disappointment in his eyes.

"I'm sorry, Apollo," Verity said with a smile. "Jacks is waiting for me."

"Jacks?" Apollo's eyes widened. "You're here with Jacks?"

Verity struggled to find the words. "Apollo, I must go now. But thank you for a wonderful evening. Your hospitality is..." She faltered, her thoughts scattered.

"My pleasure," he said smoothly, handing her the stilettos. He kissed her hand. "Maybe another time."

"Good night," Verity said softly and left the yacht without a second thought.

~

Verity and Jacks left early the next morning, and Verity was grateful. She didn't want to run into Apollo again.

After Jacks' small plane touched down on the grass runway behind her cottage in Exuma, Verity smiled at her friend, thankful for the adventure and her unflagging generosity. But something still nagged at her. *Why had Apollo spoken about Jacks as if she were somehow unworthy?*

CHAPTER 13

*V*erity had been invited to visit Rylan at his home in Moss
Town after the café closed on Saturday. He lived just a
four-minute drive northwest of Casuarina House.

She'd been on the island since June 11. *Strange that it had taken
until August 9 to finally see Rylan's house.* The thought made her
chuckle inwardly. *Maybe he saves home visits for special people.*

As her Vauxhall rolled slowly down Rylan's gravel driveway, a
black Lab named Prints trotted up to greet her, tail wagging, a deep
bark likely announcing her arrival.

Verity put the car in park, cut the ignition, and leaned forward to
take in Rylan's house through the windshield. The small white
stucco house had a black shingled roof, blending in with the homes
she'd passed on her way to Moss Town. She reached for her purse on
the seat beside her and then opened the door.

Prints was a one-dog welcoming committee, his whole back half
wiggling with excitement as he wrapped himself around her legs.
Some watchdog.

"Hey there, Prints, old buddy," she cooed in a high-pitched voice,
rubbing the dog's side before scratching behind his ears. When she

moved her hand to the base of his tail, he nearly bent in half with pleasure. Smiling, Verity cradled his furry head in her hands, gazing into his soft caramel eyes.

"Looks like you've made a friend."

She glanced up to see Rylan strolling down the short walkway, looking as effortlessly handsome as ever in denim shorts, his bare chest golden in the evening light. He greeted her with a kiss, and for a moment, Verity felt like the luckiest woman on the planet.

As they walked toward the back of the house, Prints trotted ahead. The view of the ocean and beach stretched before them. The palms and thick bushes swayed wildly in the strong wind, forcing them to raise their voices over the rustling leaves. A badminton net was strung across a sandy patch near Rylan's outdoor bar.

"Nice setup," Verity said, eyeing the nine barstools surrounding the bar. "Looks like the perfect party spot back here."

Above the bar, fisherman's netting hung with a couple of mooring buoys and colourful nautical rope. A string of patio lights was fastened under the roof's edge, casting a warm glow. But what caught Verity's eye was something more familiar—three brightly painted metal fish.

She grinned. "Ha! I see you brought a little bit of Lacey J's to your home, Rylan."

Rylan glanced at the fish adorning the back wall. "Oh, so you've been in her shop?"

"Of course," Verity said lightly, although she hoped her jealousy wasn't as obvious as a raspberry stain on a white shirt. "She told me that you two were—what was the phrase she used? *In sync.* Whatever that means."

Rylan chuckled softly, tilting his head. "Lacey's a sweetheart, a very close friend, that's all." He wrapped an arm around Verity's shoulders and pulled her in for a reassuring squeeze.

A sudden *thud* in the grassy area behind the house made them both jump.

"Whoa," Verity exclaimed, spotting the coconut that had just crashed to the ground. "Glad no one was standing under that tree just now."

"One of the hazards of tropical living," Rylan said with a laugh. "I try to have them harvested, but I guess my guy missed that one." He picked up the coconut and turned back to her. "Have you ever had coconut water straight from the source?"

Verity shook her head. "Can't say that I have."

Rylan grinned. "Well, that's about to change." He held out a hand, beckoning her closer to the palm tree. "But first—may I have the honor, my lovely?"

Rylan took her hand, and together they walked over to a dug-up area in the front yard. He pointed to the upturned soil. "And here, dearest sweetness is where I'm going to plant our tree."

"Oh?" Verity was intrigued, wondering what was the significance of Rylan's announcement.

"It'll be a flame tree, the brightest tree in the neighborhood." He flashed his dimples and put his arm across Verity's shoulders. He smiled proudly, waiting for Verity's response.

Verity was touched. She hugged Rylan and kissed him on the lips. "You are the most romantic man alive. I adore this." She squeezed him tight, bouncing on her toes like a kid about to dive into a chocolate cake.

"Let me finish, babe, he said seriously. The flame-coloured blooms will remind me of the burning love I have for you when it bursts forth in flower each spring. It'll be spectacular, like the love we share." He kissed her on the lips. "And," he continued proudly, "it's a fast grower, again like our growing love for each other. It grows about five feet every year." Rylan leaned in for another kiss and Verity turned that kiss into a meeting of lips as juicy and sweet as the watermelon growing in Rylan's garden.

As they strolled happily toward the back porch, Rylan continued, "And I know I owe you a lesson in making conch salad; it's on my agenda." He winked at Verity as he placed the coconut on a porch table and smashed it with a pointy hammer. Verity was dazzled by Rylan's magnetic charm.

Taking Verity's hand, he said, "Come on in. I'll get you a straw, and you can have a drink." Prints followed close behind as they headed into the house.

Glancing around the main living area, Verity surmised that it was a typical bachelor pad decorated without the benefit of a female's touch. *Mmm, how I'd like to be that female.* "Rylan, how long have you lived in this lovely location?"

"Since I was seven years old."

"Oh, so almost your whole life, then. Do you have any siblings?"

"No brothers, no sisters. That would've been nice." Rylan looked pensive.

And are your parents still living?"

"No," he replied, shoving a straw into the coconut and handing it to Verity. "They died together in a horrible accident on the Queen's Highway, just as they were about to turn into their driveway."

Verity's breath caught. "Rylan, I had no idea. That's heartbreaking. Seven years old; that must have been so tough."

"It sure was. I loved my parents dearly and have vivid memories of them. My dad and I used to go bonefishing when he was sober, and those times were some of the best memories I have. In the end, though, it was his drinking that led to their deaths. A dump truck rounded the curve way over the line, crashing into my dad's vehicle, which was also across the line. The police said it resulted in instant death for both of them."

"Heartbreaking. And without any siblings, it must have felt like your whole family vanished in minutes." Verity lowered her head in sadness as she listened, hearing in Rylan's voice that the pain still lingered, even after all these years. "Who raised you, then?" she asked softly, brushing her fingers gently against his cheek.

"Jed," Rylan replied, his face brightening. "Remember I told you about the man who left me George's Café?"

"Oh, yes, of course. What was his connection to your parents?"

"He and my dad were drinking buddies, though Jed wasn't an alcoholic. He did look out for my dad, and they had a lot in common. They were both born and raised here in Exuma, went to the same schools, and struggled together to make a living. And they were among the few white people on the island."

"So, he became like a father to you, then?"

Rylan nodded. "Yes. I loved him just as much as my real dad." He paused for a moment. "I was beside myself when he was diagnosed with Stage IV melanoma, knowing there was no cure."

Verity walked over and wrapped her arms around him, offering silent comfort. "Rylan, you honour his memory with the way you run the café. I can see that."

"Thank you, love. Perhaps you can see now why this island is my forever home. Everything I hold dear is right here in Exuma... and that includes you."

They sat in silence, gazing at each other for a long moment.

"You know how you've said you like the way I treat women?" Rylan asked, breaking the quiet.

Verity smiled and nodded. "Yes, I've always noticed."

"I give full credit to Jed. He treated every woman he met with the utmost respect, no matter her circumstances. He never married, but women were always tripping over each other to spend time with him."

"Sounds like he could have had his pick. Did he ever date seriously?" Verity was intrigued, especially since she had seen women fall for Rylan, too.

"Not for long. Whenever a woman started thinking about marriage, he'd gently say his goodbyes."

"A loner at heart?"

"I guess. I never really understood it myself, but I do know he was one hundred percent committed to raising me."

Rylan placed his hand on Verity's calf, his fingers stroking up past her knee to her thigh. She shivered at the sensation, her pulse quickening as she wished he would go higher. Their lips met again, and they held each other close for a long, lingering kiss. For Verity, it felt like they had reached a new, deeper level in their relationship.

Verity closed her lips around the straw, took a sip, then paused, squinting slightly. "Eeeeyah," she said, "It tastes... well, interesting." She laughed.

"Oh, I should've waited. It's much better chilled," Rylan said, taking the coconut away. He poured the remaining milk into a glass, covered it, and placed it in the fridge. As he opened the cupboard, Verity noticed two large coffee mugs similar to the one she'd bought from Lacey J., the potter. The mugs were shades of blue, adorned with the same fish motif outlined in white.

Verity found comfort petting Prints, whose gentle eyes gleamed with happiness. She smiled, recalling the yellow lab she'd once owned. "Dogs are so human," she said fondly.

"Yeah, but the best part of human," Rylan chuckled.

"I know. They offer comfort when you're feeling low. It's like they have ESP to your heart."

"True. And I can read this one's heart by his eyes. Right now, he wants you to stay here... forever." Rylan leaned in and kissed her, his lips warm and full. Prints nuzzled between them, eager to be part of the moment.

On the open verandah facing the ocean, Rylan, Verity, and Prints basked in the sunshine, shielded from the strong wind. Rylan took a swig from his beer, then turned to Verity.

"How was your weekend with Jacks?"

"So interesting," Verity said, leaning back, "being elbow-to-elbow with the rich and famous. You get a glimpse of their world in a few hours. But I'll tell you what—no amount of money could make me one of them." She shook her head and took a sip of her lemonade.

"Do you think having enough money to do whatever you want would get boring after a while?" Rylan asked.

"I'm sure it could. How many jewels can you buy before they stop intriguing you? How many yachts, vehicles, houses? How many trips can you take and still enjoy it? How many restaurant meals, each different but the same, can still bring joy? When you can have it all so easily?"

"I get what you mean, but still, I think I'd like the opportunity." He grinned.

"Sure, I loved being spoiled by Jacks and enjoying the indulgence of the ultra-rich. It was fun for a while. But I've been reading about the history of slavery on the islands here. You probably know about the long history of suicide among those who came thinking it was paradise, only to find it was too hard. Parched soil, burning sun, and rock that wouldn't yield—it hardened men, crushed their dreams. Women suffered too, under patriarchal rule and the cruelty of disheartened men. Sometimes, ending it all seemed easier than fighting an unforgiving land."

Rylan listened intently, then smiled. "You have a kind and under-standing way about you, sweetness. And I agree. One world is so far apart from the other, it might as well be different planets in the same universe."

"Enough of that for now," Verity laughed. "I want to ask you something about Jacks."

Rylan's brow furrowed slightly. "Go ahead."

"I gather she's from a wealthy family and inherited a trust fund from her grandfather. People were asking about her father at the party. But is there anything else I should know? I'm asking because I caught a strange vibe from someone there. It hinted at something sinister about Jacks. I've come to like her, and it felt weird to get that feeling."

Rylan's expression turned serious. "Just between you and me, babe, and only because you asked. And you have to swear you won't tell anyone. The only reason I'm telling you this is because, in such a short time, you've captured my heart and earned my trust."

"I'm intrigued," Verity said with a playful smile. "And no, I won't tell anyone."

"Some people believe Jacks is involved in drug running. I don't have any proof of it, and I don't like spreading rumors, but if she were ever investigated, her life with the ultra-rich would be over."

Verity blinked, piecing it together. "So, the plane...?"

"Yeah, she's a great pilot. She can land that thing on a grass runway and has flown in some rough weather. It's rumored she smuggles cocaine from Colombia every week in her Cessna 310. She pays the local fuel guy to deliver it when he refuels the airport. With cocaine selling for up to fifty grand a kilo in the States, it's no wonder money's never an issue for her."

Verity let the information sink in. "So, I've made friends with a drug runner... I thought I left that world behind when I left Vancouver."

"Maybe, and I'm sorry to disillusion you, Ver. But it could be one of those cases where ignorance is bliss."

"Yeah, what I don't know can't hurt me, right?" Verity said, looking away as if trying to distract herself from the unsettling news.

"It's like being on the party boat. You learn to turn a blind eye to certain things just so you can enjoy yourself."

"I guess." Verity couldn't hide her disappointment. She and Jacks had connected over their shared beliefs in independence and strength, overcoming relationship break-ups and deceit, and surviving when their integrity was undermined.

Rylan glanced at his watch. "I'm afraid I have to run, babe. I've got a dinner meeting tonight that I can't cancel. But maybe we can boat over to Stocking Island next Saturday and go conch hunting?"

"Oh, I'd love that! But don't you work on Saturdays?"

"Nope. Got someone filling in for me. Our time's running out, sweetness. I'd rather spend Saturday with you."

CHAPTER 14

Saturday, July 27

Verity had spent the week strolling the beach, wading into the ocean at a comfortable depth, and unwinding on the verandah. By Saturday morning, she was ready to leave for Stocking Island as planned. She hadn't seen Rylan since last Sunday, and she ached for his touch—the sensual caress of his hands, the deep, mellow timbre of his voice, the familiar, masculine scent of him.

At exactly ten, her phone rang.

Rylan's voice, rough with sleep, came through the line. "Hey, babe, I'm gonna be late. I'm sorry, slept in, but I can be there by eleven if that's okay."

Verity forced a smile. "Yes, sure. At least you're close by."

You're four minutes away. Why will it take you an hour to get here?

After Rylan finally arrived—an hour late—he swung off his motorcycle, offering Verity an apologetic grin. She huffed but couldn't hold onto her irritation for long, not when his deep, mellow voice wrapped around her like a warm breeze.

They gathered their things and headed for the dock, where boats bobbed gently in the harbor. The salty air carried the rhythmic slap of water against the pilings, and gulls dipped and glided above, their cries punctuating the lazy hum of the marina.

As they neared their small motorboat rental, Rylan called out to a bearded man who was steadying an incoming boat.

"Buzz! How's it goin'?"

Buzz glanced over his shoulder and broke into a grin. "Rylan, my man! What's up?" He turned back to the boaters, giving them an easygoing nod. "Next time, bring 'er in a bit slower, yeah?" He chuckled as the shaky boaters disembarked.

Rylan slid an arm around Verity's waist. "Taking my girl here to catch a conch and make a salad," he said, his voice brimming with pride.

Buzz tipped his cap to Verity. "Hey there, Verity," he said with a friendly nod. Then, with a smirk, he added, "If it doesn't work out, you know they serve conch salad at the Chat 'n Chill."

Verity laughed. "Good to have a backup plan."

Buzz winked. "Always."

"Right." Rylan nodded. "We'll probably make our way over there eventually. Maybe see you later?"

"Maybe. Saturday's our busiest day, but hope to catch you later. Cheers, guys."

The boat ride to Stocking Island was short. Once Rylan reached a promising spot, he anchored, pulled on his snorkel gear, and plunged into the water. Less than a minute later, he resurfaced, triumphant, holding a conch shell in each hand.

Once ashore, he smashed into one shell with a hammer, then used a knife to extract the meat, rinsing it clean. Verity watched as he struggled to tear away the last slippery bits with his bare hands. Nearby, a stingray hovered, waiting for scraps.

"Mind grabbing the rest of the ingredients from my bag?" Rylan asked. "They're in a plastic container at the bottom. There's a cutting board and some bowls in there too."

Verity rummaged through his bag and lifted out the container. "Oh, you're so organized, Rylan. Maybe you work in the restaurant industry," she teased.

"Just keep the lid on for now," he said, chopping the conch with swift precision. "I'll use it as a surface for the cutting board."

"Ah, method in your madness."

He mixed the diced conch with tomatoes, bell peppers, onion, and lime juice before spooning it into two bowls.

Verity took a bite and sighed. "Oh, Rylan. Could this be any fresher? Or more delicious?"

"Nope. As fresh as fresh can be, my love. Next time, we'll catch lobster, bring champagne, and dine in style."

Verity nestled her face into his chest. "Mmm. I like the way you think."

After cleaning up, Rylan stretched, his gaze drifting toward the inland trails. "Ready to hike over to the ocean side? We have to cross a pond first; if it gets too deep, you may have to lift your backpack over your head."

Verity hesitated. "Sure, Captain." She tried for enthusiasm, but uncertainty coiled in her stomach.

As they neared the pond, Verity eyed the water warily. She wasn't sure how deep it was, but it looked high. She clutched her backpack and waded in, following Rylan, who went ahead in case of surprises.

The water rose higher. Soon, she had to lift the backpack onto her head to keep it dry.

Panic set in as cold water crept up Verity's neck. She strained to stay on tiptoe, stretching as high as she could. Memories of drowning flooded her mind.

"Rylan, I—" She stopped. Even speaking felt like a risk to her balance.

A soft whimper cut through Verity's panic. She whipped her head around. A small figure flailed in the water, chin barely above the surface. Heart pounding, she turned fully—then saw the terror in his wide eyes.

"Swim!" she called instinctively.

"I can't!" His voice was tight with fear.

The boy's panic sent a jolt through her. She let go of her backpack and tore through the water, closing the distance between them. Wrapping an arm around his small frame, she guided him toward shore.

Rylan, finally realizing what was happening, rushed forward and pulled the boy in. Then he waded back into the pond to retrieve Verity's abandoned backpack.

Dripping, Verity turned to the boy. "Who are you with?"

The boy wiped his mouth. "No one. I—I ran ahead of my family. Thought I'd beat them to the other side."

A moment later, his parents emerged from the trees, frantic.

"He's okay!" Verity called. "The water's deeper than it looks."

She took a slow, steadying breath, trying to calm the tremors in her hands. After a brief pause, she allowed herself to be led, her fingers slipping into Rylan's as he took her hand, guiding her up the hill toward the ocean side of the cay.

"You're amazing," he murmured, pulling her close. "You put aside your fear of drowning to save that boy."

She scoffed. "Anyone would have." But deep down, she knew the truth: for her, fear had no place when someone else needed saving.

Rylan grinned. "So it was a selfish gesture, then?" he teased before tickling her, making her yelp and swat at him.

They reached the cliff's edge, and Verity inhaled deeply, letting the tension in her body ease. Below, wild waves crashed against the shore, foaming and churning in a mesmerizing display of power.

When she was ready to move on, Verity took off down the hill, racing toward the sand. Rylan followed, laughing.

Giant waves rolled in, leaving colourful seashells strewn along the beach. Verity reached into her still-damp backpack, pulled out a plastic bag, and made a game of snatching shells before the waves reclaimed them.

Hand in hand, they wandered along the shoreline until fatigue set in. They found a grassy ledge to rest, and Rylan spotted a rope swing nearby. Grinning, he walked over, hopped on, and worked it up to full swing. Verity laughed when she heard him singing *Hooked on a Feelin'* by Blue Swede.

And in that moment, she realized she was falling in love with him.

CHAPTER 15

"Let's wash off the salt; what d'you say, Ver?" Rylan called, heading toward the outdoor shower. Verity followed without protest, even though the evening air had cooled considerably.

As she soaped the back of Rylan's shoulder, her gaze lingered on his tattoo. "So, what made you decide on a starfish, babe?"

There was a noticeable pause before Rylan answered. "Oh, you know, it's the signature motif of Lacey. I think you mentioned meeting her at her shop in town. The one right beside my café?"

"That's the one," Verity replied, trying to push back her feelings of jealousy. She fell quiet, her fingers lingering on his skin before she continued, carefully choosing her words. "And... you wanted the same motif tattooed on your shoulder because...?"

Rylan turned to face her now, the spray from the shower dampening his voice. "I guess you could say it symbolizes our bond." He paused, his eyes searching hers, waiting for her reaction.

"Uh-huh." Verity's expression was unreadable, her voice a little distant. "That's nice, I guess. But... how strong would you say that bond is, Rylan?" She stood on her tiptoes, placing her hands on his cheeks to keep him from looking away, her eyes steady and unblinking.

Rylan seemed to falter, then gave a small, nervous laugh. "Hey, let's get dried off first, and I'll tell you the whole story." He pulled away from her grasp, turning off the water before grabbing a towel for each of them. Verity held her ground, forcing herself to be patient, and followed him to the verandah.

After they'd slipped into some dry clothes, they sat in the cottage living room by the shell lamp, taking some time before Rylan had to hit the road.

"Here's what happened, Verity. I guess it's almost a year ago now, last July, I think it was. We were both down at the loading dock, waiting for supplies to arrive for our businesses. It was a particularly windy day, and the dock was moving with the turbulence of the sea. We were both standing near a supporting post when one of Lacey's earrings fell in the open area between the post and the dock, created by the turbulence.

"Just as she reached down to grab it, the dock moved again, knocking her headfirst into the opening. In other words, she was positioned headfirst into the water, sandwiched between the dock and the post. If I hadn't been there to pull her out, there might have been a very different ending."

Verity tried to picture the scene. "Oh, how frightening for both of you. Was she injured?"

"She had a few painful cuts and scrapes from the barnacles clinging to the post as I pulled her out, but the worst part was how shaken up she was from the whole experience. I mean, think of it...happily shouting over the wind one minute in anticipation of our packages arriving, and the next minute submerged under water, lodged between two moving structures threatening to crush you at any moment."

"Thank goodness you were there, babe. I'm sure Lacey is forever grateful for your rescue that day." Verity tried her hardest not to sound sarcastic. Although she felt sympathy for Lacey's dramatic plunge, a flicker of jealousy simmered beneath the surface—one she hadn't fully acknowledged until now.

"Yes, she's forever grateful, it seems," Rylan hesitated before continuing, then, in a quieter voice, said, "She calls me her shining star. That's actually where she came up with the idea for the starfish motif for her business, and of course, she wanted me to have it tattooed on the back of my shoulder so that, in her words, "You'll always remember that your star performance that day saved my life.""

Verity listened, then said, "Of course, she wanted that. Yes, and what else did she say?"

"Nothing else, really, I mean, nothing relevant to our own relationship, sweetness."

Verity didn't feel satisfied; she just felt unsettled. "Are you seeing Lacey, Rylan?"

He nodded, looking at her directly. "We see each other now and then, Ver, but we're close friends. What about you? Are you dating anyone back in Vancouver?"

They hadn't discussed lovers, past or present, until now. "Um-hmm. Just for a few months before I decided I needed a change of scene, I started dating someone, yes."

"I see." There was a slight shift in his expression—*relief, maybe?* "Even though we get so wrapped up in each other that it can feel like there's only us, well, we've both lived a bit of life, haven't we?" Rylan commented.

"We have," Verity conceded, although she still felt uneasy about the Rylan/Lacey relationship. She recalled the look in Lacey's eyes when she told Verity they were "in sync."

"And, Rylan, I'll be honest with you." Verity glanced down, thinking about how to phrase her thoughts. "I thought I found my true love in Charlie, my ex, and when I found out that he was cheating on me, well, I can't even begin to tell you how devastating that was for me."

Rylan pulled her close. "I'm so sorry to hear that, babe. That must've shattered your world."

Verity glanced up at Rylan, appreciating his empathy. "That's it in a nutshell, Rylan, and you can probably appreciate that I don't want to make the same mistake again."

"Understandable, babe. Sometimes we need a trial run before striking gold," he said.

Verity's mind raced. *Let's hope it's not fool's gold.*

Even though it was barely six p.m., Rylan had prepared Verity for the fact that he wouldn't be sleeping over that night. Something about things he needed to take care of before the start of the week. Rising from the sofa, he tilted Verity's chin toward him, and pressed his lips gently to hers, drawing her into a warm embrace. As he slowly deepened the kiss, Verity felt as if he were reaching deep into her soul, his presence filling her completely.

"Please believe me when I say I'm in love with you, babe. That means you and only you. No one else."

Verity was stunned. *You love me?* Her eyes locked on his as she absorbed his words. Placing her hands on Rylan's face, she gazed into his blue eyes, certain that her own conveyed every ounce of what she felt at that moment.

"Rylan, I love you too, so much." As they shared a passionate embrace, Verity thought back to her doubts about love at first sight. *This isn't just lust. Men don't say the three words women long to hear unless they mean it.*

Reluctantly, they broke apart, and Rylan stood, pulling Verity into one last embrace. He kissed her forehead gently before stepping back, his expression soft but serious.

Verity watched as he grabbed his jacket and headed for the door.

She listened as his motorcycle rolled down the driveway onto the Queen's Highway, heading northwest toward Moss Town.

REGARDLESS OF RYLAN'S sensitivity to her feelings of insecurity, Verity grew increasingly edgy as the night wore on. And even though he had proclaimed his love for her, saying she was the only one, she still couldn't shake certain images from her mind. The way he had kissed those two women in colourful shifts the day she went for lunch at the café, the way Lacey's dreamy gaze lingered when she thought of Rylan and their connection, the memories of Rylan rescuing Lacey, the starfish tattoo, the metallic fish, the pottery mugs, and her own delayed rescue as Rylan laughed and chatted with the woman in the boat. Verity felt like she was tallying incidents in her mind, afraid to see the total.

Turning the key in the ignition, Verity asked herself, *Am I crazy? Am I so jealous that I have to go check up on him?* Her mind flashed back to her time at Hillside College when her amateur sleuthing had uncovered important details that helped prevent further crime. *Maybe I should have gone into detective work.*

Parking her car some distance away from Rylan's house, Verity entered his driveway, prepared to flee if Prints started barking. The lights were off, and Rylan's bike wasn't in the yard. His garage door was shut.

Disheartened, she turned and walked back to her waiting Vauxhall, her heart sinking. She was convinced Rylan wasn't home, even though she had no concrete proof—other than the heaviness in her chest.

CHAPTER 16

Sunday, July 28

There was a vague suggestion that they might get together on Sunday and look for lobsters. When Verity hadn't heard from Rylan by eleven that morning, she called him. She let the phone ring seven times before hanging up. Then, in case she'd misdialed, she called again, letting it ring for five. Still no answer.

Verity needed some time to get her head straight. Everything had happened so fast between her and Rylan. *Was there any such thing as love at first sight?* She had always thought it was a crazy notion. She was pretty sure it took time to fall in love.

But every time she saw him after that first night, it only reinforced the idea that it *was* love at first sight. Because things had grown more passionate and real, one night building on the next.

As she tried to sort her feelings, Verity's mind flashed to her dear Aunt Lucy, who had left her a fortune. When Aunt Lucy was alive, Verity could confide in her about anything. She imagined explaining her feelings about Rylan to her, recognizing that no one else could offer the same level of understanding and genuine support.

She tried to imagine what her aunt might say: *True love was built on mutual trust, genuine care, and support—not something determined by a first kiss.* Alone on the verandah beneath the swaying casuarina trees, Verity shook her head in confusion.

She walked barefoot into the kitchen to get some food. A piece of watermelon, a small bowl of last night's leftovers, and a slice of homemade chocolate cake.

Back on the verandah, she continued her analysis, as if trying to piece together a puzzle. *Maybe, as time goes by and you still share that same passion...* Verity's stomach fluttered as she relived Rylan's goodbye kiss the night before. *The passion that surpasses mere physical craving—maybe that's when you know you've struck gold.* She thought deeply, taking a long sip of water.

Verity was on a roll. *A passion that matures into an undeniably deep union of souls—yes, souls, not just bodies. Maybe then you know it was love at first sight all along... but could you have known for certain the first time you met?*

With the last bite of cake and one too many thoughts, Verity needed a break. She stripped off her clothes, grabbed a towel, and dashed to the beach—completely ignoring the advice never to swim alone.

Throwing down her towel, she sprinted into the water—only to be hit by a huge wave at the worst possible moment. It catapulted her back to shore, leaving her sputtering and coughing. Once she caught her breath and stood up, she made sure to stay well away from the surf. Then she looked out at the sea, laughing aloud as she imagined the ocean had spat her out for her stupidity.

A rustling in the bushes nearby caused Verity to turn her head. A young man was doubled over laughing—probably at her pathetic aquatic skills, or more likely, at a nude woman frolicking alone in the waves.

She skipped back to the cottage, still laughing at her impulsiveness, but not caring. Jumping into the outdoor shower, she thought, *No matter what happens, this is exactly where I want to be.* She relived the thrill of showering with Rylan, swimming with Rylan—everything with Rylan.

By the time Verity settled into her favourite spot on the verandah, she thought she had it figured out. *True love might be a mystery, but there were signs.*

THE NEXT DAY, Verity decided to check the post office just in case Rick had written. She had kept her promise to herself not to call him but had sent a postcard after her first two weeks away.

At the post office, she immediately recognized Rick's handwriting on an envelope dated July 7—three weeks ago.

With no other plans for the day, Verity walked down to the marina, greeted Buzz, and found an empty dock to sit and read Rick's letter.

DEAREST VERITY,

Just writing to say I miss you but you already know that. Even though we were just getting to know each other, joined by a common purpose, there was an undeniable attraction between us. Undeniable.

Don't get me wrong, Ver. I wanted this getaway for you just as much as you did. I could see you needed it—that's an understatement. And you so deserved it. Sometimes it takes a getaway to help put things in perspective. I hope that when you look back on our relationship, you will realize just how special it is.

Do you have telephone service at the cottage? I'd love to hear your voice again; as it is, I hear it only in my dreams or in those fleeting moments that come out of the blue and take me away from what I'm doing. Those are the most telling times, Ver, because my inner voice is sending me a message.

And now, in this letter, I'd like to send a message to you, Ver, in four simple words:

You're everything to me.

Not pushing at all, but do you know when you'll be coming back? Truly not pushing. Just wondering.
All my love,
Rick XOXO

VERITY READ the letter a second time, then folded it and placed it back in the envelope. She gazed out at the water, her thoughts a swirl of emotions. She had enjoyed her time with Rick, brief as it was, and appreciated his genuine and caring nature. However, recent experiences had shifted her perspective.

The gentle lapping of the waves against the dock mirrored her inner turmoil, each ripple a reminder of the connection she both valued and questioned. Uncertain of her path forward, Verity acknowledged that returning to Vancouver—and to Rick—was a possibility she couldn't fully embrace.

WHEN VERITY ARRIVED BACK at Casuarina House, she decided to go for a walk and try to relieve the heaviness that Rick's letter imparted. She headed left, toward Jacks' property and, thinking this might be a good diversion, decided to take Jacks up on her invitation to walk the property at any time.

Walking across the scruffy ground, Verity eyed the plain, gray cottage ahead. The scene contrasted so sharply with the world of the rich and famous, that she couldn't understand why Jacks didn't choose something more upscale. *This place isn't even on the scale.*

She walked along the paved walkway that circled all around the structure and, reaching the backyard, saw that Jack's plane was gone, as she expected it would be. Even though she hadn't been given a key, she tried the doorknob to Jack's living space anyway. She wasn't sure why she did that. *Not sure why I did that—just making sure, I guess.*

She walked to the back of the building again, looking out onto the runway and the field beyond. She headed out toward the field and, seeing big, empty spaces between the seagrape bushes at the back of the property, decided to explore.

Did the locals party here on weekends, too? She'd be able to tell right away, but there was no evidence of firepits, discarded bottles, or other debris. The Queen's Highway was on the other side of the bushes, and Jacks' driveway was about thirty feet northwest of where Verity was standing.

She headed in cautiously, giving herself room to escape in the unlikely event that she needed to. The crime rate was very low on the island, Rylan had told her.

A clunking sound that seemed to come from the direction of Jacks' house stopped her short. She wasn't sure if she also heard voices over the offshore wind.

She found an opening in the bushes that made a good peak hole where she could watch comfortably and clearly. Verity positioned herself to face the house. She caught sight of what looked like two men, youngish, walking toward Jack's house from the ocean side. One stationed himself at her front door while the other walked around to the back as if looking for something or someone.

As Verity kept a close eye on him, movement at Jack's front door caused her to look there. She saw the other man raise his leg and kick open the front door. The violation made Verity's skin crawl.

She held her breath as she watched the second man come in from around the back of the house and join his partner inside Jacks' living space.

Her pulse quickened. She shifted her focus just in time to see the first man lift his leg and kick the door open. A chill ran down her spine Her mouth was dry as she waited, making sure not to move and stay hidden by the bushes. She forced herself to remain still, crouched low in the dense greenery. If they looked her way, would they see her?

She quelled her impulse to run to the highway and try to find someone who might help. *But help do what? She'd already experienced the attitude of the local police chief.*

Through the windows, she could see the men moving about throwing things here and there as they ransacked the room. She felt sick watching damage being inflicted on her friend's possessions. Verity also kept an eye on the driveway in case any accomplices might enter the property that way.

A black dog came bounding across Jacks' property. At first, Verity thought it was just another stray—but no, she recognized him. "Prints," she whispered in horror, thinking her cover was blown. Instead, Verity watched the two men exit the cottage and walk away hurriedly, carrying only a small bag. She was sure it was the same one they had arrived with.

'Prints, good dog,' she murmured. 'You scared them away.'

Prints approached Verity, wagging his whole back half, jubilant to have followed her scent right to her exact location. The dog's presence gave her the courage to move ahead.

No sooner than she'd started, she and Prints were alerted to the sound of an old SUV rattling down Jacks' driveway. Verity froze, wrapping an arm around Prints. The vehicle rolled halfway in, then abruptly backed out. She exhaled. *Nosey tourists, maybe.*

She looked ahead, hoping to see Rylan. As she crept closer to the shore, she saw the two men motoring their dinghy toward a small cabin cruiser anchored nearby.

She crouched down, again hidden by some bushes, not wanting to be seen. By the time she reached the beach, the men were motoring out to sea in their boat.

Verity sat down on the breakwater and placed her head in her hands. She felt exhausted. *How can I do what's best for Jacks?*

When she finally mustered the strength to walk back, she called for Prints, and together, they returned to Casuarina House.

Rylan, napping in an Adirondack chair on the verandah, woke with a start when Prints licked his hand, causing Verity to smile. She was warmed and relieved by Rylan's presence.

"You look pale," Rylan said, his expression shifting to concern. "Everything okay?"

"No," she said, "but how about you listen in while I call the useless police, so I don't have to tell the story twice." This was more a statement than a question. Verity sounded like she just wanted to get the job done and unburden herself of unpleasant thoughts.

Rylan hugged her and stroked her back, moving his hand up and down, up and down. His caring eyes showed his concern for Verity. "Sure, babe. Let me get you a glass of water."

Before stepping inside, Verity crouched to hug Prints once more. Then she kissed him on the nose.

ABOUT THREE HOURS LATER, the police officer knocked on Verity's front door. He'd investigated the crime scene and then came to talk to Verity and make a report.

"After answering questions like, 'How do you know Jacks? What were you doing on the property? Do you have any idea why anyone would want to break into her house?' Verity was starting to zone out.

The officer, however, was persistent. 'Do you know anything about the secret room behind the bookcase?'"

Verity went pale. 'What?' she stammered, a deep furrow creasing her forehead.

"Yes," the officer affirmed. "Looks like your friend Jacks had much to hide."

Verity tried to look surprised without showing the true level of her concern for Jacks. "I, uh,..." she began. "No, I don't know anything about that. This is new information to me."

She glanced at Rylan, who had turned to look out the window. He'd expressed concern since overhearing Verity's conversation with the police, worried that a search of Jacks' property might not be in her best interest. But it was too late. All he could hope for now was that the officers would live up to their reputation of being as 'useless' as Verity claimed.

The officer nodded his head and handed Verity his card. "If you think of anything else that might be helpful, just give us a call, okay?"

"I will," said Verity weakly, and she moved aside as he headed out the door.

The silence of the room seemed heavy after the officer left, giving Verity and Rylan a chance to digest what had just happened. The life-changing consequences of a conviction for a drug-related crime.

Rylan's soft voice broke the silence. "Hey, sweetness, would you like me to show you more of the north island next Sunday?"

Verity smiled, feeling his desire to cheer her up. "Rylan, I'd love that. What's on the north island?"

"Oh," he teased, "let me surprise you. Just bring your bathing attire and a big appetite."

"Sounds marvellous, babe," Verity rested her head on Rylan's shoulder. Better than marvellous. But what are you doing on Saturday?"

"I'm flying to Nassau for a meeting with other café owners. I went last year—it was good. Learned a few things, met some nice people."

Verity knew another week without Rylan would drive her crazy. 'Do you think you could pop by on your way home sometime during the week? We could have dinner together if that works."

"I'd love that, Ver. How about Wednesday?"

"Perfect. That'll give me some time to get my head together after seeing Jack's place trashed. You'll be my mid-week treat."

~

Verity smiled as she watched Rylan and his motorcycle cruise down her gravel driveway after work on Wednesday. She realized that even three days apart seemed too long to be away from him. *Always come toward me, my love, never away from me.*

They enjoyed a stir-fry of fresh veggies Verity bought from one of the stands in town that same day. She served it on basmati rice, adding some smoked tofu for herself and chunks of medium-rare sirloin for Rylan.

When it was time to leave, Rylan drew her in close and kissed her passionately. Verity melted into the power of his embrace. She couldn't wait to see him again on Sunday.

CHAPTER 17

*S*unday, August 4

Feeling the wind push her hair away from her face, Verity imagined it sweeping away the stress of the Sunday before.

Sitting on the back of the motorcycle, Verity relished the feeling of wrapping her arms around Rylan's waist as they sped toward Williams Town, a 45-minute trip.

Rylan slowed to cross the bridge to Little Exuma. Verity recognized the spot where she'd gotten lost trying to find Casuarina House for the first time, having to turn around and redirect herself toward Georgetown.

Along the route, on the right-hand side of the road, Verity noticed a group of five or six Black women dressed in their Sunday best, even though it was still Saturday. *A special event today, maybe.*

A woman dressed entirely in pink stopped to smell what seemed like a wild rosebush before heading up the steps to the church. Verity strained to catch the harmonious sounds of gospel music floating from the church and asked Rylan to slow down.

Heading east toward Tropic of Cancer Beach, they turned where a telephone pole with two blue reflectors marked the spot. Like

Cocoplum Beach, it was known to locals but nearly unknown to tourists.

The road to the beach entrance was rough, and Rylan had to slow down, dodging potholes and mud puddles. After parking the bike, Rylan and Verity grabbed their bags, and just as they headed down the short stairway to the beach, they paused to view the imaginary Tropic of Cancer meridian running along the steps.

Rylan knelt near the painted line and, anticipating Verity's reaction, explained, "This marks the northern boundary of the tropics." Verity was surprised and wanted to ask someone to take a photo of them together at the landmark, but there was no one in sight. Rylan took a picture of Verity to send to her parents.

"Yet another pristine, secluded beach," Verity exclaimed. As they approached, she looked left and right along the entire stretch of sand.

"It's a mile long," Rylan said. Small dunes dotted the shore, with a cove to the right. He pointed toward it and added, "Let's put on our snorkel gear and see if we can find some pretty fish over there."

They walked across the white sand toward the distant cove, set their gear down, and slipped into their snorkeling equipment. Rylan wore fins, and Verity donned her water shoes. It was another warm day, the mild breeze carrying a few voluminous white clouds across the sky. But the water was calm, and the cove was protected, making it easy to swim and snorkel. Verity's thoughts briefly flashed back to Gina holding hands with Rylan that day off the party boat.

When Verity spotted the blue-green, silvery metallic hues of a barracuda, she immediately forgot about Gina. As before, its long, narrow body swam by without a glance, not giving Verity a chance to feel nervous.

With her mask submerged in the water, Verity found herself swimming right through a school of zebrafish, their black-and-silver bodies darting all around her. One bumped her forearm, giving her a small scare. *Keep those needle-sharp teeth away from me.*

Before long, Verity peeked out of the water to check where Rylan was. She spotted him—lying still in the water, face down, clearly watching something.

She swam over to him and, just as she arrived, caught sight of a large stingray with white markings, a variety she hadn't seen before. But as soon as Verity neared, the stingray swam away in the opposite direction.

They snorkeled together for a while longer until Rylan began pointing excitedly at something in the water. A turtle swam past, momentarily blocking Verity's view, but then she saw it: a pufferfish. Its sharp spines radiated from its inflated body. Verity and Rylan kept their distance, knowing the pufferfish could release a toxin harmful to humans. Soon after, two colourful parrotfish swam by, followed by a bright orange and white clownfish.

They both noticed the sudden appearance of a large, white-spotted eagle ray gliding just above the shallow ocean floor, barely moving. Rylan found Verity's hand and gently led her away. Verity had read in her guidebook that the eagle ray's whip-like tail was armed with two to six venomous spines.

Back on shore, they dried off, drank some water, and snacked on spears of pineapple. Looking beyond the cove toward an abandoned house high on a cliff overlooking the ocean, Verity was intrigued. *Is the whole island abandoned?*

Just in case anyone did come along, they hid their backpacks in the bushes before hiking through the rest of the cove. Purple sea fans were strewn about the sand, some blown against the rocky bank. They climbed over some rocks and continued uphill until they reached the abandoned house.

In the dilapidated shed, a rusty old Sunbeam car had been left behind. Verity wondered if there might be more objects inside the house, just waiting to be discovered. *If they left behind a car, what else did they not want?*

The rusty screen door was partially torn, its edges hanging loose from whatever had once held it in place. Looking inside, Verity could see a mess of discarded clothing, dishes, a radio, paperback books, an old washstand, old magazines, and a shell collection. Verity was eager to sort through the cluster of seashells lined up on the bottom shelf of an old cupboard.

Rylan stepped ahead, opened the screen door, and walked in. Verity was more cautious, carefully studying the structure for holes in the floor, broken glass (there was plenty of it), and anything that might fall from the ceiling.

Since Rylan had moved through without mishap, she decided to follow. The house smelled musty, despite the fresh sea air blowing through the open spaces.

As she poked around, Verity felt an odd sense of intrusion. Yes, it was clear the place had been abandoned for some time, but still... she was trespassing.

She wondered who had lived there. Judging by the fashion magazines, it was likely a woman—and the large, stiff white shirt and the man's shoes suggested a couple. There were no children's toys, but maybe they'd taken them when they left. With only one bedroom, Verity assumed the couple lived alone.

"Why would anyone abandon such a beautiful spot? And it looks like they left in a hurry," Verity mused aloud.

"Maybe they were criminals who escaped to Exuma with their drug money and bought a beautiful house on a cliff overlooking the ocean," Rylan suggested.

"Maybe," Verity replied thoughtfully. "Or maybe these people were involved in the slave trade. Maybe they were slave owners, and eventually, they were run out of town." She smiled to herself, pleased with the backstory she'd created. And now, she didn't feel so guilty rummaging through the place.

She had become an avid sheller and could identify most of the specimens on the shelf. But when she came across a pinkish, ribbed shell, she paused, amazed at its exquisite design. She couldn't believe someone would leave behind such a beautiful specimen.

First, she admired the shell's beauty, then ran her fingertip over the ribs. Finally, she picked it up, studying it from every angle, holding it up to the light—careful not to drop it. *This is a gem!*

And then, guilt started to creep in. Sort of.

Spotting what was left of a roll of toilet paper on the floor, she grabbed it, unrolled what remained, and wrapped it around her treasure. She tucked the package into her running shoe and zipped up her backpack.

Just as she was about to leave, Verity noticed an old, yellowed newspaper on the kitchen table. The front page read, in large, bold letters: *"Racial Tensions, Unfair Labor Practices at Exuma Resort Hotel."* The article was dated May 5, 1957.

Verity was intrigued by the paper being left in plain view, as though it had been read the very day the owners fled, leaving everything to deteriorate with the house.

She skimmed through the article and quickly grasped the context. *Bahamian workers were forced to yield to overbearing expatriate workers who allegedly told Bahamians their skin color made them inferior. Furthermore, Bahamians with certain complexions weren't allowed to work in certain areas of the resort.*

"Hmm, interesting," Verity thought. *I wonder if this has anything to do with why this house was abandoned.* Her inner sleuth kicked in, and she promised herself she would investigate further.

Verity folded the yellowed newspaper and stuffed it into her backpack.

Reinvigorated by her discovery of the stunning seashell, Verity left the musty house with a big smile on her face and rejoined Rylan outside.

"Pretty nice view, huh?" he said with a smile, wrapping his arm around her waist.

"Let's buy this place and fix it up. What do you say, babe?" Verity joked.

Rylan kissed her on the lips and said, "I could live anywhere with you, my love, but this place creeps me out."

Verity's stomach rumbled, prompting Rylan to ask if she was

ready for lunch. They made their way back to the motorcycle, heading slowly down the road away from the beach, their wet bathing suits flapping in the breeze.

∼

Seven minutes later, they parked the motorcycle on a patch of hard-packed dirt by the side of the road. To their left stood Marley's Bar and Grill, and to their right, Mama's Bakery—two simple wooden structures perched on a rocky rise, both serving the community for the past twenty-three years, Rylan said.

"Galy owns the diner, and her mom runs the bakery," Rylan explained. "We could grab some of their bakery treats for later if you want. Her rum cake's to die for."

The scent of fried food made them both quicken their pace toward the wooden benches surrounding the bar. Bright lime green, orange, and blue added a splash of colour to the oceanfront eatery, with picnic tables offering views of the ocean and a thatched-roof area providing shade for those who sought it.

"Rylan! Good to see you. How've you been?" Galy greeted Rylan with a wide, friendly smile, her gleaming white teeth sparkling in the sun. She turned to Verity, offering a smile just as welcoming, though a little smaller.

Setting two plasticized menus on the bar, she added, "The Kalik's been sittin' on ice for two hours." She tilted her head and raised her brows in a playful challenge.

Rylan glanced at Verity. "That's the local brew, babe. Want to try one?"

"Sounds good," Verity said with a nod, skimming through the menu.

Galy set down two frosty bottles of the golden lager. Verity took a sip, savouring the refreshing taste. "Ah, that hits the spot. What do you recommend for lunch, Rye?"

Rylan didn't even bother with the menu. "Grilled lobster, no question. It's served with caramelized onions, rice and peas, and coleslaw. I pretty much always get it."

"Mmm, sounds great."

"And Galy's husband, John, goes fishing every day," Rylan added with a proud grin. "So the food is always fresh."

Verity admired Rylan's island pride. She loved how he spoke about the place like it was part of him.

When Galy brought over two generous plates of grilled Bahamian lobster, Verity couldn't wait to dig in. The moment her teeth sank into the tender, flavorful fish, she looked at Rylan with wide eyes.

"This is wildly delicious, Rylan! And this has to be the most amazing surprise of my life, babe." She leaned over and kissed his cheek, even though her mouth was full of food. "You're the best. I love, love, love you for sharing this day with me. I'm the luckiest girl in the world right now."

Rylan's eyes twinkled with pleasure, and his dimples flashed as he took another swig of Kalik.

"You know," he said, "if you want to do a bit more snorkeling, we could check out some different fish on this side of the island. And, by the way, see over there?" He pointed across the water to a distant point. "That's where Jed loved to go bonefishing."

Verity paused, her fork halfway to her mouth. "Bonefishing? Is that kind of like fly fishing? Only with bones instead of flies?" She laughed a little too loudly, realizing she hadn't a clue what bonefishing was.

"Ha, that's funny, Ver. But bonefishing isn't a technique—it's a type of fish."

Verity laughed again, this time a little embarrassed. "Oh! I had no idea. Never heard of a bonefish."

"They like shallow water, so Jed preferred wading out to fish rather than using a boat."

"Did you fish with him a lot?"

"Yeah, a lot. And I'll tell you, those bonefish are tough. One time we got caught in a strong tide, and man, that was a game-changer."

"How so?" Verity asked, intrigued.

"Jed hooked a big one near the mangroves. Less experienced anglers might've backed off or lost the fish in the thick cover, but Jed knew how to work the openings in the mangroves. If a fish charged the fly, he'd try to lead it out of cover before it had a chance to take it."

Verity listened with interest, even though she wasn't a fisher herself. She could tell the story was dear to Rylan's heart.

"Then, when he had the fish hooked solidly, he'd raise the rod high and hard, lifting the fish's head out of the water," Rylan continued, checking to make sure Verity was still following. "See, if the tail's up instead of the head, you're done. The fish can't swim backward, only forward, and when the head's up, the kicking tail works in the angler's favour, pushing the fish away from the mangroves."

Verity leaned her shoulder into his with a playful grin. "Okay, I'll always make sure your head's up so you can propel yourself toward me, not away."

Rylan smiled but stayed focused. He wasn't done yet. "Here's the clever part. You need to lead the fish away from cover. Our instinct is always to pull against the fish, but in this case, he's already followed your fly out of the mangroves, so he's moving in the direction you want. You need to swing the rod in the direction he's facing, which is away from the mangroves."

"The fish will almost always panic and swim away from the safety of the mangroves into open water. That's when you ease off the pressure and let him run until he's on the reel. Then you follow him into the open water and land him." Rylan's expression was triumphant, as though he could picture the capture in his mind.

Verity smiled, teasing, *Okay, once I lure you in, I need to keep pulling you my way. When I think I've got you hooked, I'll let you run for a while. Then, when I know I've reached my limit, I'll reel you in, claiming my prey.*

"I'm glad you have such vivid, fond memories of Jed, Rylan. I wish I could've met him," she said, reaching over and squeezing his thigh.

After praising Galy's cooking, Rylan paid the bill, and they walked hand-in-hand toward the outdoor seating area and up onto the rocks above the sea. The wind had picked up, sending their hair flying in every direction, but the Caribbean sun still warmed their skin, calling them back into the water.

They reached a sandy spot, and before getting his gear on, Rylan left to use the washroom. Verity pulled her mask over her head, adjusting it for comfort and a perfect seal, then slid the mouthpiece in and pointed the tube toward the back of her head. She stepped into the shallow water, careful around the scattered rocks beneath her, and put on her water shoes.

A flash of silver caught her eye—she saw a school of fish darting by. Without hesitation, she slid into the water, her body sinking smoothly as she positioned herself face down, her eyes scanning for movement beneath the surface. She froze in place, unsure of what she was seeing.

The fish swam toward her, and as she turned to head back to shore, a sharp pain shot through her foot.

Panicking, she flailed in the water, trying to push her way toward land, grateful that she hadn't strayed far without Rylan. Her feet touched the ground, but before she could make it to shore, another agonizing bite pierced her lower leg.

Verity screamed, the pain unbearable, and hobbled toward the shore, desperate to get out of the water. She tore off her snorkeling gear, frantic, her eyes searching for help.

Rylan heard her screams carried by the wind and raced toward her, shouting over the roar. "What happened?" His eyes followed the trail of blood streaming down her leg and over her foot. Glancing at the water, his heart froze when he saw about a dozen reef sharks still circling nearby.

Rylan shouted for Galy while trying to comfort Verity. Within minutes, Galy raced to the scene with her first-aid kit as Rylan carefully carried Verity to the seating area. He gently laid her on her back, elevating her leg on a nearby wooden bench. Galy swiftly removed sterile pads from the kit and applied pressure to Verity's foot while Rylan pressed another pad firmly against her leg.

Verity's tears tapered into soft whimpers and shuttering breaths as the comfort of caring hands eased her panic. She tried to focus on the care she was receiving, pushing the attack from her mind. *You're okay now. You're in safe hands.*

The wound on her leg required a second pad, which Galy applied over the first until the bleeding slowed. Verity kept her eyes on Rylan, his calmness a small comfort as he pressed the pads together with steady hands. Still, the pain raged like fire in her foot and leg, as though they were being sliced open by knives.

Galy dressed the wounds temporarily, making sure they were stable enough to move Verity to the emergency clinic in Georgetown. She then hurried to the bakery, soon returning with a bottle of ibuprofen, a glass of water, and a blanket. "This'll help reduce the swelling, darlin'," she said gently, handing Verity the pill and the water.

Rylan tucked the blanket around Verity, looking into her eyes with a soft yet firm expression. "You're probably in shock, sweetheart. Just try to relax. Close your eyes and sleep if you can." He stroked her head with one hand while caressing her shoulder with the other. Verity felt comforted by the warmth of his touch and the reassurance in his voice. Tears of gratitude and pain slipped down her cheeks, but when she closed her eyes, the images of the attack rushed back, making her snap them open again.

Rylan bent down and kissed her cheek. Galy, who had been watching quietly, spoke up. "Rylan, I think it'd be best if you take Verity in my car. I'll send Leah with you to help keep her leg elevated on the way."

Rylan's relief was evident. He stood, giving Galy a heartfelt hug. "You're an angel, Galy." He pulled back and smiled, his voice lowering. "Your calmness... it made all the difference. I was falling apart inside."

Galy gave him a humble smile, glancing at the ground for a moment before jumping back into action. "The car's ready. I'll grab a pillow and another blanket, and maybe an upside-down drink carton to elevate her leg in the back seat."

Once they were settled in Galy's car, a young girl approached the window, introduced herself as Leah, and announced that she'd be sitting in the back with Verity. Her smile was bright and confident, proud to help.

All thoughts of Mama's rum cake were forgotten as they sped toward Georgetown and the small medical clinic next to the bank.

CHAPTER 18

*S*unday, August 4 – Monday, August 5

Verity was lucky. The wounds were only punctures—no torn flesh, no damaged tendons or nerves. She could still move her leg and foot, still feel them.

Back safe in Casuarina House, the worst of the pain had finally eased after hours and stronger analgesics. Leah had caught a ride back to Williams Town with her dad, and the house was quiet.

Even in her semi-alert state, Verity felt the comfort of being home with Rylan—like a warm fire on a cold day. As she drifted toward sleep, Rylan's voice pulled her back.

"You know, reef sharks don't usually attack humans. Any idea what might have drawn it to you, sweetness?" He didn't want to stir up the trauma, but he needed to know—so he could protect her in the future.

"I was thinking about that too." Her voice was soft, groggy. "D'you think I still had the scent of lobster on my skin?"

Rylan considered that. "Maybe. You'd think it'd wash off in salt water, but who knows." He fell quiet for a moment, then said carefully, "You know, they go for blood. Any chance you're on your period?"

Verity stilled. Her groggy eyes met his. "Oh."

Her lids grew heavy, sliding shut, shielding her from frightening thoughts—at least for now.

RYLAN DROVE Galy's car back to Williams Town and handed her the keys.

"Galy, you're a lifesaver. I can't thank you enough for everything today."

He gave her a quick hug and then filled her in on Verity's condition. Galy beamed when she heard there was no nerve or tendon damage and that, in time, Verity would heal well.

"As for the emotional damage," Rylan added, "it might take a while before she's comfortable getting back in the water."

The grill had closed for the night, but Rylan noticed the bakery lights still glowing. He grinned. "I don't suppose Mama has any of her rum cake left?"

Galy laughed. "Come on in. You know Mama always has rum cake on the go."

As they walked toward the bakery, Rylan glanced left, his mind flashing back to the horror of the afternoon. He inhaled deeply, then exhaled, steadying himself before pushing open the door for Galy.

The scent of warm spices and baking sugar wrapped around him the moment the screen door banged shut. The air inside was thick with humidity, and the long wooden table—covered with a colourful oilcloth—displayed fresh goods. Against the far wall sat the same small gray loveseat, draped with an old beach towel, just as it had been for as long as Rylan could remember. Beside it, a tall stainless steel cart held baking trays and dishes.

Nothing had changed in the twenty years he'd been visiting Williams Town, and that was part of the charm. On busy days, overflow customers perched on the loveseat, while others lined up out the door. During quieter moments, Mama herself would sometimes take a breather there, always happy to pose for a photo when asked. Over the years, she had become something of a local celebrity, beloved by both residents and tourists.

Hearing voices in the front room, the eighty-year-old woman emerged from the kitchen, wearing her signature cap and apron. Best of all, she wore her warm, familiar smile.

Rylan barely had time to greet her before she pulled him into a hug.

She pressed a gentle hand to his arm. "I heard about what happened, child. That poor girl. I want you to know I've been praying for Verity's healing."

Word of the rare shark attack must have spread fast. Mama shook her head, her face lined with sorrow. "The whole community's shocked. We're all thinking of her."

Rylan nodded, touched by her kindness. "That means a lot, Mama. Thank you."

He knew she'd be up before dawn, filling the bakery with the scent of fresh bread, doughnuts, pastries, and, of course, her famous rum cake. Once, when she was younger, she had driven to George-town each morning to sell her baked goods from a van. The boating crowd around Elizabeth Harbour had devoured them, some saying her treats were the highlight of their trip. Now, her granddaughter Leah—the same Leah who had sat beside Verity in the car that after-noon—ran the bakery van instead.

Mama's soft brown eyes twinkled as she wiped her hands on her apron. "Now, what can I get for you, Rylan?"

"I was thinking a little rum cake might help lift Verity's spirits."

Mama's eyes crinkled with warmth. "Certainly, my pleasure."

She crossed to the stove, retrieved a warm pot of rum sauce, and set it on a trivet. "Chocolate?"

"Oh, definitely the chocolate," Rylan said, then grinned. "Let's make it a whole cake. I have a feeling Verity's going to want more than one piece while she's recovering." He chuckled. "And, well... you know I might sneak a slice or two myself."

Mama laughed, reaching for a long, thin needle to pierce the cake. Slowly, she spooned the warm rum sauce over the surface, letting it soak deep into the sponge.

Rylan thanked her again before tucking the cake carefully into his motorcycle carrier. Then, with one last wave, he kicked off toward Casuarina House, the scent of rum and chocolate trailing behind him in the night air.

VERITY JOLTED awake at 3:00 a.m., a sharp, searing pain ripping through her wounds.

"It's like the sharks are biting me all over again," she gasped. "Rylan, it's unbearable—like I'm being sliced with a knife."

Rylan was out of bed in an instant. He grabbed her pain medication from the nightstand, squinting at the directions in the dim light. Because she'd slept so long, she'd missed a dose. Cursing under his breath, he quickly twisted off the childproof cap and shook out the prescribed pills, pressing them into her trembling palm along with a glass of water.

She swallowed them and then let out a shuddering breath.

Wanting to soothe her, Rylan found some soft music to play and eased onto the bed beside her. Gently, he ran his hand over her back as she lay curled on her left side, keeping pressure off her injured right.

Little by little, the tension in her body eased.

Forty-five minutes later, her breathing grew steady. The pain had finally let her go.

Rylan didn't move. He just kept his hand on her back, listening to the sound of her breathing as the night stretched on.

CHAPTER 19

*M*onday, August 5

As Verity started to feel better the next week, she decided to research the abandoned house they'd explored high above Tropic of Cancer Beach.

Near the town hall in Georgetown, she found a small library. Favouring her right foot, she made her way inside and approached an elderly Black woman sitting behind the desk.

"Excuse me," Verity said. "I'm interested in finding out the history of an abandoned house we saw near Tropic of Cancer Beach."

The woman considered her for a moment. "Uh-huh. You mean the one up on the cliff?"

Verity couldn't tell if her expression was exhaustion or the weariness of someone who had answered this question too many times before.

"Yes," she replied. "Is there a history of the area here? Or is there somewhere else I might find information?" She kept her tone polite despite the woman's cool demeanour.

With a heavy sigh, the woman pushed back her chair and slowly stood. She walked over to a set of books displayed along the side wall, scanning the shelves until she found what she was looking for.

"You might find something in here," she said, handing the book to Verity before returning to her desk without another word.

Verity hobbled to a nearby table and flipped through the pages. A few moments later, a woman—mid-forties, with warm brown eyes—leaned down and spoke quietly.

"I overheard what you were asking about, and I might be able to help," she said with a friendly smile. "My name's Dee."

Verity gestured for her to sit. "I'd love to hear what you know."

"My mother used to talk about that house. It's a well-known story among Bahamians," Dee began. "I was about twenty-three when all this went down."

Verity stayed silent, listening intently.

"The people who lived there were Americans from Seattle. The man ran the Exuma Resort Hotel—back when it was at Hooper's Bay, where they're building the new Island Resort Hotel now."

Verity nodded. She knew the spot; she passed it every time she drove into Georgetown.

"A lot of Bahamians worked at the hotel," Dee continued. "They were glad to have jobs, but the way they were treated..." She shook her head. "The owner worked them to the bone for low wages, made sure they did all the dirtiest jobs, and kept the easier work for the white staff."

Verity's stomach tightened. "Blatant discrimination."

"Sure was," Dee said with a sneer. "Didn't sit well with the locals—or even some of the white folks who lived here."

Verity leaned in. "So how does this connect to the house?"

Dee rested her forearms on the table and lowered her voice. "By the time this hit the newspapers, people were already up in arms and planning retaliation. Everyone knew where the hotel owner lived, but instead of storming the place outright, they gave him and his family until noon the next day to leave the island."

Verity exhaled. "That explains why the house looks like they left in a hurry. There was even a car still in the garage."

Dee smirked. "Oh, they probably had two."

"What happened to the hotel?" Verity asked.

"The media attention put a target on his back. Authorities started looking into things, and turns out, he built his little empire on drug money. Ended up in prison. The government seized everything."

"So that house has been sitting abandoned for nearly twenty years?"

"Yep." Dee sat back. "There were plans to turn it into a water sports facility, but things here are either boom or bust. Not enough money to see it through."

Verity pictured the house again, recalling the way she had imagined it restored, with her and Rylan living there. She shivered.

"Even if I could buy the place," she murmured, "I don't think I could live with its history hanging over me. That kind of past—it leaves a bad feeling in my heart."

Dee nodded solemnly. "Some places carry a weight you just can't shake."

Before heading home, Verity decided to drop by Lacey's store to see if she carried any seashell guidebooks. She was curious about the unusual ribbed shell she'd brought back from the abandoned house —it wasn't in either of the books she had at home.

A note on the door read, *Back in 15 minutes,* but it didn't say when the note had been written. Verity smirked to herself. But she was getting tired now. Hobbling around took more energy, and she was still recovering from her ordeal. *Did anyone ever really get over a shark attack?*

Hoping to recharge, she headed to George's Café for some tea— maybe even a quick visit with Rylan, if he wasn't too busy.

As soon as she stepped inside, the door jangling behind her, she spotted Rylan and Lacey at a table near the back, deep in conversation. Rylan looked up immediately, pushed back his chair, and stood, his expression shifting to surprise.

"Ver," he said, crossing the room to greet her. He pressed a quick kiss to her lips.

Lacey twisted in her chair to see who Rylan was talking to, then gave Verity a pleasant smile before taking a sip of coffee.

"I wasn't expecting to see you today," Rylan said. "How's your foot?"

"No, I guess you weren't," Verity replied, offering him a half-smile. She lifted a hand in a small wave toward Lacey. "Hi, Lacey."

She shifted her weight carefully. "It still hurts to put full pressure on my right foot, so I'm walking a bit lopsided. But it's a huge improvement from before, so I'm grateful."

Stepping closer to Lacey, she asked, "Do you carry any seashell identification books in your shop?"

"I sure do," Lacey said. "Let's go over now and have a look. How's your leg?"

"Better, thanks. Healing well, I guess."

Verity turned to Rylan. "I want to identify that unusual ribbed shell I... you know, found near Tropic of Cancer Beach." She hesitated, surprised by her reluctance to mention the house now that she knew its history.

"Oh," Rylan said, "you mean the one from the abandoned house?"

Verity stiffened. Instead of answering, she turned back to Lacey. "Yes, please, I'd love to take a look now, if you don't mind."

AT LACEY'S SHOP, Verity found a comprehensive guide filled with full-colour pictures. Later, back at the cottage, she stretched out on the couch, propping up her right leg comfortably, and took her time studying the book.

When she finally found the shell, she let out a quiet *Oh. No wonder I didn't recognize it—it's not even from the Bahamas.*

The shell belonged to a species of sea snail commonly known as harp snails or the ribbed harp. "*Harpa costata,*" she murmured into the quiet of the cottage. Skimming ahead, she read that it came from the waters off Mauritius. *Where's that?* She traced the tiny map with her fingertip. *Off the east coast of Africa.*

Her thoughts flicked to the abandoned house. *Well, I suppose a wealthy resort owner-slash-drug dealer could afford to travel.* But she refused to let the shell be tainted by its previous owner. *It's not its fault.*

Lifting the ribbed harp, she ran her fingers over the delicate ridges. *How could something as unassuming as a snail create something so beautiful?*

Strangely, the thought carried her somewhere deeper. To the absurdity—the cruelty—of people deciding which kinds of beauty were worthy. *All living things are born beautiful.* But that beauty could be marred—by circumstance, by other people who had been damaged themselves. Hurt people hurting others. A cycle that never seemed to end.

She didn't want to follow that train of thought any further. Setting the shell aside, she made herself a gin and tonic over ice, willing herself to push both the thoughts—and the image of Rylan and Lacey together—out of her mind.

Don't mix painkillers with alcohol.

She hesitated for only a moment before taking a sip.

CHAPTER 20

Tuesday, August 6 – Sunday, August 11

VERITY SLEPT in later than usual the next morning, still drained from yesterday's excursion to Georgetown. She took her time getting up, then made herself a breakfast-for-one—French toast with the last drizzles of Canadian maple syrup and a strong cup of coffee.

Lately, her appetite had been stronger. *Maybe my body's just looking for some rebar to shore up my recovery.*

Seeing the maple syrup nearly gone reminded her to check the calendar. *How much longer do I have?* Though she'd initially left her return date open-ended, she'd finally booked a flight—Monday, August 19. *Otherwise, I might never leave.*

She had commitments in Vancouver. Her parents were there. And Rick.

Verity hadn't replied to Rick's letter. They had agreed—no contact. She had left everything and everyone behind, good and bad, for a few weeks to clear her head. To let the ocean's salt water rinse her soul clean.

And yet, his letter had unsettled her. *When someone says, "You're everything to me," you can't pretend they don't exist.*

She crossed the kitchen to check the calendar. A large red heart circled August 19. She counted the days aloud—twelve left, with the last one a travel day. *Less than two weeks.*

A familiar dread settled in her chest. *How will I say goodbye to Rylan?* The only thing that would get her through it was knowing they'd see each other again.

Shaking off the thought, she decided to focus on today.

Her foot still wasn't ready for flip-flops, but her heart longed for the beach. The sun would do her wounded leg some good. She pulled on a pair of running shoes and stepped outside, determined.

Walking the beach again felt like freedom. She moved slowly, cautiously, relishing each step. The sand shifted under her feet, challenging her balance, but she felt strong.

"Hey, stranger!" Gina's voice rang out from up the shore.

Verity hesitated. She wasn't sure she had the energy for Gina's unfiltered personality. Still, she gave a small wave and made her way over.

"Looks like you need a sit-down, hon," Gina said, setting out two chairs in the sand.

Verity sank into one gratefully, surprised by how good it felt to rest.

"What happened to you? Did you have an accident or something?"

Verity blinked. *Gina doesn't know?* News usually spreads fast on the island. Verity wondered if Gina had been holed up in her cottage or on a bender.

She recounted the shark attack, her voice steady at first—but as she spoke, the memory surged back, raw and vivid. Her eyes stung with tears. "Okay, I need to change the subject. I'm trying to forget those terrifying moments."

"Sorry, hon," Gina said quickly. "Alright, here's some news, in case you haven't heard."

She launched into a story about the break-in at Jacks' cottage, not realizing that Verity had been the one to report it.

When Verity filled in the missing details, Gina's eyebrows lifted. "I see. The officer didn't mention you reported it. But he did knock on my door, asking if I'd seen anything."

"What did you tell him?"

"First off, I didn't let him in—obviously. Didn't want him sniffing around in case he caught the wrong scent if you know what I mean." Gina smirked. "So, I stepped outside, closed the door behind me, and told him about the boat I saw anchored just offshore. Not something we see too often in this area. Then I saw a dinghy push up onto the beach."

Verity straightened. "Did it seem suspicious?"

Gina shrugged. "Not suspicious, exactly. Just... out of the ordinary."

BACK IN THE COTTAGE, Verity sat in the warm evening air, reflecting on an earlier conversation with Rylan. Saturday nights were their time to get together—he'd said it was easier after the café closed at six. It felt like she was holding her breath all week, waiting for the weekend.

I'm obsessed. His charisma, his passion, his empathy, his confidence, his dog. She closed her eyes and sighed, imagining his lips, his gentleness, his skilled touch.

HEARING Rylan's motorcycle in the driveway on Saturday, August 10, at eight p.m., Verity whispered to herself, *Less than two more weeks to go.* But that didn't matter now. *Just enjoy tonight before it slips away.*

The night was warm, with a gentle breeze and the sound of waves lapping against the shore. Verity mixed three different rums in her shaker and served Bahama Mama cocktails, with pineapple wedges as garnish.

When she handed Rylan the tall glass loaded with ice, he seemed distracted by her lips. He hesitated, just a moment, before taking the drink. Then, he leaned in and kissed her.

"Thanks for the drink; it tastes good," he smiled, holding her gaze so intently that it took her breath away.

They didn't last long outside—midges found them after ten minutes, driving them back indoors. Standing in Verity's bedroom, Rylan looked down at her with such tenderness, his eyes smiling with pleasure, that she felt cherished. He stood so close that she could feel his heat, and hear his breath.

Is he imagining what it would be like to spend the rest of our lives together? She could only hope.

Rylan brushed his lips against hers before closing his eyes and kissing her gently. Verity felt the intensity of his desire as his kiss deepened, lingering at first, savouring, then growing urgent.

He pulled back the bed covers and set Verity gently onto the bed. Propped up on her elbow, she watched Rylan undress, a movie she could watch again and again. As he pulled his white tee over his head, exposing his chest, Verity grinned. "I love the way you look," she murmured, her eyes tracing the lines of his chest.

He flashed her a dimpled smile, his gaze softening as he took in her words, his focus entirely on her.

Verity's pleasure surged as he slid out of his shorts and joined her in bed, careful not to bump her wounds.

"Mmm, you're exquisite," she moaned, rolling on top of him. Verity sighed. "God, I just love your body."

Rylan's sensual touch sent Verity into another world. His easy arousal made her feel like the sexiest woman alive. Hours passed in a blur of heat and connection, blending into one, as Verity found renewed energy wrapped in his arms. "Oh, Rylan," she cried, moving with him, lost in their rhythm.

"Yes," was all Rylan said, over and over, his voice hoarse with pleasure.

When it was over, Verity lay there, still breathless, struggling to find words.

THEY HAD dinner on the verandah, and as Rylan slid his hand up her thigh, she was sent spinning. He touched her between her legs, making her shiver with pleasure before they'd even gotten to dessert. *I'll have another serving of this, please.*

Verity was in ecstasy and couldn't imagine life without Rylan.

As the evening wound down, Verity was distracted by the flapping of wings from a creature that looked like a moth, but much larger.

"Rylan, is that a bat?" She shrank back toward him, not taking her eyes off the mottled brown creature.

"Oh, no," Rylan replied, somewhat mockingly, she thought. "That's a black witch moth."

"Why 'oh, no'?" Verity asked, her voice tinged with curiosity.

Rylan chuckled softly. "People on this island believe the black witch moth brings death or misfortune wherever she lands. She's obviously well misplaced here at Casuarina House." He tucked his face into her hair, breathing in the scent of her honeysuckle cologne.

"That's creepy," she said, watching the moth continue flapping around the porch light.

"Yeah, I guess. Mexicans believe if someone's sick and the moth enters the house, the person's going to die. Other versions say it has to touch all four corners of the room for it to work. And if it flies over your head, they think you'll lose your hair."

Verity pushed against Rylan, moving farther from the moth. "How do you know it's female?"

"The white bar across the wings is a dead giveaway." He smiled, looking at the moth. "And the wingspan—must be nine or ten inches across—is a strong indicator she's female."

As Verity studied the creature in the light, she noticed flickers of iridescent purple and pink colors. "You're right, my love. There's no place for a doomsday moth anywhere near Casuarina House."

They stepped into the bedroom, closing the screen and glass door behind them, locking it against any creatures of misfortune.

CHAPTER 21

*S*unday, August 11 – Monday, August 12

After Rylan left on Sunday evening, Verity lingered on the verandah steps, her thoughts drifting back to Saturday night. The memory of his touch wrapped around her like a whisper, drawing her into a world she cherished even more now that time was slipping away.

Alone in her kitchen on Monday morning, Verity admired her new coffee mug from Lacey J's, holding it up to examine the bottom. There, embossed in the unglazed clay, was a starfish motif, along with the year it was made. *A nice touch.*

Only seconds later did Verity realize that the motif was the same one she'd seen on the back of Rylan's shoulder. *Rylan, the Rescuer.* The discovery deepened her confusion about his feelings for her. Perhaps the coffee mug was no longer her favourite. Perhaps she'd leave it behind when she returned to Vancouver.

After her second cup of coffee on the verandah, Verity walked down the white stone path, barefoot, in nothing but her bikini and wide-brimmed sunhat. She never tired of the simple joy of walking the beach, searching for sea treasures, a habit she'd resumed now that her recovery was progressing so well. Before the shark attack, this had been her morning routine, and she loved the lightness of it—the freedom of the beach, with no agenda other than to collect unique seashells.

Today, she found an unexpected cone-shaped shell just as she began her walk. Cautious after reading the warnings in her seashell book, she bent down to inspect it, wondering if it might be poisonous. Unsure, she used the brim of her hat to scoop it up and placed it on a ledge to retrieve on her way back.

As she headed northwest, she caught sight of a large bird perched on the top of a tree along the beach. White-breasted with dark wings—*Could it be an osprey?* Excited, she continued toward it, her eyes locked on the bird. Standing under the tree, Verity gazed upward as the bird gazed down at her. When it spread its wings wide, a chill ran through her, and her heart skipped as the bird seemed poised to attack.

Standing there, bare feet in the sand, her heart raced. As her survival instincts kicked in, she grasped her hat by the crown and waved it wildly, stretching as far as she could toward the bird. She held her ground for what seemed like an eternity—then, just as suddenly as it had swooped toward her, the bird veered off toward the ocean.

Her heart hammered in her chest as she processed the idea that she'd scared off the giant bird. She thought about how vulnerable she'd felt, standing there in just a bikini and hat, yet she couldn't deny a surge of pride at her quick thinking.

Wanting to shake off the unsettling moment, she hurried back to the cottage to collect herself, forgetting to retrieve her cone.

After gulping down a glass of cold lemonade, Verity set out once again, this time wearing running shoes and carrying a sturdy walking stick. Heading in the same direction as before, she spotted

Gina sitting in a beach chair outside her cottage, waving as Verity approached.

"Mornin', sugar. You're a little late this morning, aren't you?"

Verity nodded, a wry smile tugging at her lips. "Ha, well, I started at the same time as usual, but I had to fend off an osprey attack, then went back to the cottage to regroup."

"Oh, yeah, I read about a photographer being attacked. Pretty rare, though. But who wouldn't be attracted to such a beauty?" Verity wasn't sure if Gina was mocking her or just jealous of her relationship with Rylan, but she didn't care anymore. She'd long since decided to tolerate Gina's passive-aggressive behavior to keep the peace. It seemed like avoiding other people's agendas was impossible, even on a remote island in the Atlantic.

Perching on Gina's rock wall, Verity changed the subject. "Have you ever been to Abaco Island? I was thinking of taking a ferry over there."

Gina's expression softened as she pondered. After a moment, her lower lip curved slightly. "Abaco... oh, yes, you'd love it. When were you thinking of going?"

"Soon, I suppose. I could use a break, frankly. I read a little about it in a tourist brochure."

Gina's enthusiasm grew. "You can rent a bike and cycle to beaches with gin-clear water. Or take a ferry to Turtle Cay, Elbow Cay, or Treasure Cay—each one's a perfect day trip. Gorgeous beaches where you can sip a pina colada, listen to live music, and watch the sunset. Hey, I could have my Aunt Ruthie put you up for a few nights if you'd like."

"Thanks, Gina, but I've been considering The Sandpiper Resort at Marsh Harbour."

"Good choice," Gina nodded. "You can get the ferry right in front of your hotel there. Just a word of warning—sit at the back of the ferry if you don't want to get wet." She grinned. "Makes me want to pack a bag myself, but then there's the construction crew coming tomorrow. Who knows how long they'll be here?" She raised her brows, lips curling into a playful smirk.

"I think I'll book a room at The Sandpiper. A change of pace, not that I need a change from paradise, but maybe from one paradise to another," Verity said, laughing. "And Jacks has kindly offered to fly me there today before heading back to Nassau. I think I'll take her up on that."

As Verity headed toward Casuarina House, Gina went inside and turned on the radio, where severe storm warnings for Abaco and the surrounding area were being announced. "I bet Jacks wants to high-tail it back to Nassau before the storm hits," Gina muttered to herself.

Back in the cottage, Verity ran through her reasons for wanting to go to Abaco. She was tired of worrying about Rylan's feelings for her, wanted to see another island before her return to Vancouver in eight days, and needed a break from thinking about shark attacks.

She packed for a three-night stay. With Monday night already here, that left full days on Tuesday and Wednesday, and she'd book a return flight for Thursday. Rylan would be at work, so her absence on Tuesday and Wednesday would be of little consequence. Perhaps she wouldn't even mention it... *well, maybe if he calls,* she thought.

CHAPTER 22

*M*onday, August 12 – Friday, August 16

Jacks placed Verity's suitcase in the second-row seats. Verity couldn't help but think of Rylan's story about drug traffickers in Colombia transporting small quantities of cocaine in suitcases on their way to the United States. She glanced back and noticed a brown tarp covering the third-row seats.

"Is that where you hide the bodies, Jacks?" she joked.

Jacks let out a hearty laugh. "That's where I keep my stash."

Verity raised an eyebrow. *She's probably not kidding.* "Well, looks like you've got enough there to keep the party boat stocked for the next year."

They both laughed as Jacks fired up the engines, and the whirring propellers drowned out any further conversation.

After taking a taxi from the airport to The Sandpiper, Verity made her way to the top floor and unpacked the few items she'd brought for her short stay. Her room on the third floor overlooked the harbor and the resort's private beach. With the windy conditions and rolling surf, she was relieved to see that the resort had two outdoor pools, along with a restaurant and bar. She was also glad that Jacks had gotten her there in good time.

From her window, she watched the sailboats rock gently in the marina, while the turbulent water crashed against the shore and stretched out toward the distant cays. Verity figured she'd better go swimming before the weather turned rough. Though the pool was an option, nothing compared to the ocean. She changed into her bathing suit, threw on a coverup, grabbed a towel, and headed down to test the water.

The sheltered harbor was warm and inviting despite the wind in her hair. She waded in up to her waist, savouring the sensation of the water. That's when she spotted it—a bright yellow seahorse. *What's this little beauty doing so close to shore?* Verity wondered if it was ill.

Eyes wide with disbelief, she extended her little finger toward the seahorse's tail. To her surprise, the tiny creature wrapped its tail around her finger and began to sway back and forth. She brought her hand closer to examine it, marvelling at its scaly exterior and the exquisite design of its horse-like head. *So precious.*

Not wanting to keep it out of the water too long, Verity gently released the seahorse into the harbour. Instead of swimming away, it remained motionless, almost as if it were waiting.

Puzzled by the seahorse's strange behavior, Verity mentioned it to the woman at the front desk when she returned to the lobby.

"Creatures know when something's up," the woman said, recalling Verity's check-in.

"Oh? What's up?" Verity asked, curious.

"There's a storm warning for the islands. It's supposed to be severe, but we'll see how it goes."

~

By Tuesday evening, rain pelted down in torrents, bouncing off the concrete walkway along the harbour. Verity sat at her table on the open terrace of The Boathouse Restaurant, gazing out at Marsh Harbour and the array of moored boats bobbing up and down. The bright yellow table linens fluttered gently in the breeze.

She'd chosen black fin grouper for dinner and noticed the servers quickly gathering up menus and stemware as soon as orders were taken.

"A bit breezy tonight," Verity commented to her server, who steadied the stem of her melon martini on the tray.

"Yes, seems like the storm is building," the dark-haired woman replied as she set the light green cocktail down.

"Oh, is a storm forecast?" Verity asked, hoping to find out more information.

"Yes. It's supposed to be a severe storm," the server said.

Verity nodded thoughtfully. *Maybe that's why Jacks seemed in such a hurry to get back to Nassau.*

"Well, I'm from Vancouver," Verity added, "and we do get a lot of rain, but not usually like this."

The server laughed softly. "Storms are different here, that's for sure. And when there's a severe storm, that could turn into a hurricane pretty quick." Her eyes widened, and she emphasized the point by jutting her chin forward.

"Huh. A hurricane. I haven't experienced one of those yet. I wouldn't even know what to do."

"Oh, no worries, ma'am. We Bahamians have ridden out a lot of hurricanes, and we lived to tell the tale." She smiled and walked away, adding, "I'll be right back with your grouper."

As the server left, Verity mulled over the conversation. *Why hadn't I bothered to listen to the news on the kitchen radio before making this trip?* She thought about how her behavior had shifted since arriving in Exuma—how she'd embraced a sense of newfound freedom and been swept up in the joy of discovering her island paradise.

She remembered Gina's excitement about Abacos and how the woman had practically urged her to come. Normally, Verity was quick to give people the benefit of the doubt. But now, considering everything happening here in Abacos, she wondered if Gina had simply ignored the warning, just like many others.

Verity took a deep breath, her gaze drifting to the rain-slicked harbour. *Maybe living in the moment isn't always the best plan. Maybe it's time to start paying more attention.*

By Wednesday afternoon, rain pelted down forcefully, causing concern. She watched it pool everywhere. Through the curtain of water, she could see the sea surging, its waves battering the shore. Her excitement about experiencing island culture was now tempered by a growing sense of apprehension.

By Wednesday evening, the storm had fully developed, and all flights in and out of the island were cancelled.

Verity sat in a plush chair, her legs stretched out on the footrest, a mohair blanket draped over her for warmth and comfort amid the unfamiliar circumstances. She gazed out the picture window, wondering how much worse the storm would get and when she might finally be able to return to Exuma.

She dialed Rylan's number to let him know where she was and that her return was uncertain until the storm passed. But there was no answer.

WHEN VERITY LOOKED out her window on Thursday, her scheduled departure day, the rainfall hadn't let up. The wind howled through the windows, and palm fronds were flung violently against the glass.

At breakfast, murmurs rippled through the patrons, all voicing concerns about possible flooding, cancelled flights, and early check-outs. Verity's attention was drawn to the outside, where a battered piece of metal flew through the air, signalling an increase in wind speed. The absence of smiles on the guests' faces mirrored the growing anxiety that hung in the air as time passed.

After breakfast, Verity headed to the lobby for a closer look. Her stomach churned like the turbulent sea as she watched the swells rise to heights she hadn't seen before. It seemed as though the waves were crashing more frequently, and she began counting the seconds between them. *One thousand one, one thousand two...* she calculated that a wave hit every nine seconds. She knew for sure she wouldn't be flying out today.

Back in her room, Verity dialed Rylan's number again, praying he'd pick up. On the third ring, doubt crept in, and she wondered who else she could call if he didn't answer. Her only other options were William, the cottage caretaker, and Jacks, but she knew Jacks wasn't home.

"Hello?" Rylan's deep voice was a lifeline to Verity, but her relief was fleeting.

"Rylan, it's Verity. I'm in Abaco at The Sandpiper Resort."

"Abaco?" Rylan's voice shot up, his concern clear. "Has the hurricane hit yet? Babe, what are you doing there?"

"It's about to hit, that's what they're saying, and Rylan, I'm scared to death. I'm a babbling mess. People keep talking about 'the eye of the storm.'"

"Verity, stay right where you are. What floor are you on?"

"Third, the top floor."

"You need to move down to the lowest floor. Now. I'll do my best to reach you. Just hold tight. In the meantime, I'm calling my friend Joe Barton. He'll help you unless he's already evacuated."

"But, Rylan, how can you get here in this storm? All the flights are cancelled."

"You leave that to me, Ver. I may not make it, but I'm sure as hell going to try." With that, Rylan hung up.

Later that evening, Verity was still in the dining room when the power cut out. For what seemed like an eternity, everything plunged into darkness, amplifying her fear of the unknown. When the backup generator kicked in, the lights flickered back on, but Verity's nerves were already frayed. She made her way to her new room on the first floor, where people were rapidly checking out, and plenty of rooms were available.

~

BY FRIDAY MORNING the ocean swells seemed bigger still, and mounds of debris had collected on the ground, with more blowing through the air. Verity had tossed and turned all night, making it even more difficult to stay calm.

With mounting apprehension and fear, Verity watched in astonishment as people fought determinedly against the raging wind, suitcases in hand, struggling to reach their vehicles. Getting the doors open presented additional challenges that seemed impossible to conquer.

Is this the grand exodus? Should I be doing the same? But where would I go? A deep frown furrowed her forehead as she studied the battering waves and fallen trees. All she could do now was hope that Rylan's friend Joe Barton would arrive soon.

With the phone lines down, she was unable to contact Rylan any longer. Verity longed for reassurance in the comfort of his arms. She imagined the sensation of his warm breath close to her ear, his luscious lips melding into hers, his loving touch caressing her breasts, her hips, her thighs.

Garden sculptures in the hotel garden lay in shambles, and plant pots were broken and scattered about. The hotel staff had removed garden furniture and tied the outbuildings with a rope secured to rebar.

By 8:40 a.m., Hurricane Judith hit Abaco with full force. The intense winds plowed through, building a wall of seawater that slammed into the coast as the hurricane made landfall. Ocean swells had risen to about twenty feet, someone said, pushing inland for unforeseeable distances taking roofs off houses, denting trailers, and causing dangerous debris to fly through the air. A mobile home had been thrown on its side, crushing a small car beneath.

Verity trembled in fear as she grabbed her packed suitcase and joined a small crowd of people crouching low, clutching their belongings and seemingly waiting things out. *At least, if the roof blows off, I'm not on the top floor.*

"Wasn't there an evacuation order?" Verity shouted out to anyone listening.

"Yes, but we ignored it," said someone she recognized from the front desk.

"But, why?" asked Verity helplessly.

And then the awful truth. "Because we've been through hurricanes so many times and never had to evacuate, despite government warnings to do so. But this time, we were wrong."

The room fell silent for a moment as the truth sank in. Their quiet only amplified the sounds of the raging wind, the surging sea, and the frantic shouts from the near distance—voices of those caught outside, helpless against nature's fury.

Hunkered among the crowd in the lobby, Verity kept her suitcase and raincoat tucked in close to her body. She felt sick at the thought of Rylan travelling by sea, but she knew, without a doubt, that she had no influence over his decision to go.

The hurricane was mind-numbingly loud and destructive, even through the boarded-up windows of the hotel, causing Verity and those around her to fear for their lives. People talked of seeing post holes filled with water where wooden posts had been set, the posts themselves turning into deadly torpedoes destined to hit the closest target.

A limb from a toppled tree had pierced the wall of a nearby house, someone said, and Verity imagined it wouldn't take long until the house succumbed to the water, making it even more vulnerable in the wind. She hoped that the family had long evacuated.

She listened as people tried to alleviate even a fraction of their fears as they told and re-told some of the horrors they'd witnessed.

An abandoned car with all the windows blown out, the rear door ajar, sunk into the sodden earth. The body of a small dog lay lifeless by the entrance steps to the hotel. With increasing sadness, Verity listened as a young woman talked about the aviary full of beautiful tropical birds now gone, with hundreds of birds now lost.

The severe flooding, torrential rainfall, and furious winds produced a tornado. It hit the hotel's backup generator, someone said, taking out the emergency elevator and leaving elderly people stranded on the third floor. Volunteers doggedly walked up and down six flights of stairs, rescuing those who could walk and carrying those who couldn't make it on their own. Sandbags placed around the harbour were rendered useless, disappearing into the flood.

Verity's peripheral vision caught the figure of a sturdy Black man pushing open the door sheltered by the solid, covered breezeway attached to the side of the hotel. With the wind changing erratically, he must have chosen the perfect moment to slip into the lobby—the only entrance not barricaded against the relentless wind and rain.

His voice boomed, even against the noise of the exterior forces. "Verity Child. I'm looking for someone called Verity Child. Are you here, Verity?" His voice, although somehow calm, seemed unsurprisingly urgent.

"Yes, that's me," shouted Verity, rising and turning toward the man as he walked quickly toward her. Feeling the stares of others nearby, Verity didn't know what to expect.

"I'm Joe, sent by Rylan to bring you out this hellhole." Verity hardly had time to process the fact that her attempted rescue was about to take place. Her heart ached for those who would be left behind in the lobby.

Joe grabbed her suitcase and instructed her, "Do up your raincoat and follow me. My truck is right outside here, but look out for flying debris. I'll open the passenger door for you. But I'm going to leave your suitcase just inside the door until I can wrestle it safely into the truck."

Verity zipped up her coat, tied her hood in place, and hurried cautiously toward the side door, following Joe. But before Joe could open the door, they were intercepted by an older man of African descent who looked up at Joe and shouted, "Please, can me and Tilley come with you, Joe?"

Joe and Verity halted momentarily so Joe could address the man's plea. "Mike," he shouted close to the man's ear, "I can't, or I would. You know that. But two more men are coming with us, so there's not enough room."

Mike looked down at the floor. "Just thought I'd ask, Joe. You be safe now," and he started to walk away.

"Wait, Mike." Reaching deep into his pants pocket, Joe found a key and handed it to Mike. "Look, take this and, if you can make it to my place...never mind, you and Tilley can cram into the back with my dog and the suitcases if you can manage it 'til we get to my place."

The look of gratitude in Mike's eyes was palpable. He took his wife Tilley by the hand after they zipped up their coats, grabbed their bags, and headed out the side door, following Joe and Verity.

Verity said nothing as Joe took her hand and guided her to the truck. There was no time for further talk. Joe forced the passenger door open and helped Verity up to the high seat while Mike and Tilley worked their way into the back.

Joe's white terrier wagged his tail and barked as Mike brought the dog onto his lap. "It's okay, Sammy," he said, and he wrapped one arm around Tilley, who'd stacked two bags on her lap while she and Mike maneuvered their legs around the other bags.

Joe slammed the truck door shut once Verity was safe inside, then returned to the hotel lobby to get her bag. She watched as someone wrestled to close the hotel door after Joe exited with Verity's suitcase.

Struggling to pull the driver's side door open, Joe placed Verity's suitcase in the space behind the front seats, where his terrier now stood, looking anxious. Joe got himself behind the wheel and wrestled with the ferocity of wind and water to pull the door shut.

He'd taped the windows of his truck as well as he could against possible breakage. The truck was already turned around, facing away from the hotel, so now he drove forward onto the road, steering away from hazards as he drove the four of them plus one scared dog onward away from the coast.

THE STORM OUTSIDE WAS RELENTLESS, but inside the truck, Verity could feel a fragile sense of safety as Joe navigated through the devastation. The wind howled, and rain lashed against the windows, but the truck's sturdy frame offered a small but significant barrier between them and the chaos.

The truck's headlights cut through the darkness, momentarily revealing debris scattered across the road. These brief flashes illuminated the storm's devastation but did little to dispel the pervasive sense of uncertainty and danger.

Verity's heart hammered in her chest, not only because of the storm but because, finally, she was on her way out—away from the island, away from the fear that had been gripping her since the storm's early whispers.

Beside her, Sammy, Joe's little white terrier, let out a nervous yelp, his fur standing on end as the truck lurched over a particularly large branch in the road. She reached down to pat the dog's head, offering comfort where she could.

"Hold on, it's going to be rough," Joe shouted over the roar of the storm, his voice steady despite the panic-inducing conditions.

Verity nodded, feeling her body tense in anticipation with every bump, every turn that took them further from The Sandpiper Resort. She glanced back at Mike and Tilley in the rearview mirror, their faces pale but grateful. Mike squeezed Tilley's hand, giving a small nod of reassurance.

The highway, or what was left of it, seemed to twist and bend under the weight of the storm, and Verity could feel the truck fighting the wind with each passing mile. She wanted to reach out and touch Joe's shoulder to thank him, to say something—anything —but the words were stuck, swallowed by the vastness of the storm and the weight of what she had just escaped.

She thought of Rylan again, wishing with everything in her that he could be there, that he could somehow make it to her side. But there was no signal, no way to contact him, and the thought of him out there, somewhere, trying to reach her—amidst all the chaos— was almost more than she could bear. She closed her eyes briefly, focusing on the steady hum of the engine and the comforting presence of those around her.

"Hang in there, Verity," Joe said again, his voice now more of a quiet encouragement than anything else. His knuckles gripped the steering wheel, and though he was in control of the truck, there was an underlying strain in his demeanor, as if every second counted.

Verity nodded, her lips pressed tightly together. There was nothing she could say, nothing that would change the reality of the storm or the uncertainty of what would come next. But at that moment, with the world outside crashing down, it was enough to know she wasn't alone.

And maybe, just maybe, there was still hope—hope that she could survive this, and that, when the storm finally passed, Rylan would be waiting for her.

CHAPTER 23

*I*n the heart of the storm, Rylan and Buzz were tossed about in Buzz's aging fishing trawler, battling monstrous waves driven by 170 mph winds and relentless torrential rain. The storm's fury intensified rapidly as the trawler pitched and dove through white-capped waves, reaching heights of up to 90 feet, eventually tilting to a perilous 45-degree angle before slowly righting itself near the harbour.

The ferocious wind was so powerful that it forced Rylan's eyelids wide open, making it nearly impossible to see land through the sheets of water. The hurricane's deafening roar rendered any attempt at communication futile. Clinging desperately to the railing, they fought to keep from being swept overboard, witnessing the main pier at the Sandpiper Hotel torn apart. Sunken and battered boats collided in the harbour, some hurled onto the shore amid the fury of uprooted palm trees. Hurricane Judith's devastation was unmistakably evident.

As Buzz cut the trawler's engine to navigate through the marine graveyard of wrecked vessels, he and Rylan exhaled in relief, the boat finally coming to a halt amidst the debris. "This is it," Rylan shouted, unsure if Buzz could hear him over the storm's roar. "Let's get off this damn thing while we still can." Struggling against the wind, he stepped onto the wreckage, using the remnants of boats for support as he made his way toward shore.

Once ashore, Rylan glanced back to see Buzz close behind. "Your trawler saved our damn lives," he grinned, bowing his head and raising his arms to shield himself from the onslaught of wind, rain, and flying debris. Crouching low, they clung to anything they could find, dodging debris from all directions and battling gusts strong enough to lift them off the ground and slam them back down.

FOUR PEOPLE and a white terrier named Sammy arrived at Joe's boarded-up shack in about fifteen minutes. Rows of sandbags surrounded the house, and nothing was left to blow away that hadn't already. The shack was more inland but still well in harm's way.

"Okay, you have the key, Mike. The house is supplied with enough food and water to sustain you for two weeks. Everything's secured, including the roof. There's a chainsaw in the inner room if you have to cut down any dangerous fallen trees, but surely I don't need to tell you not to risk your life going out into this mess. You'll find flashlights and batteries, a small camp stove, pretty much everything you need to ride out this monster hurricane."

"God bless you, brother," Mike managed, his eyes brimming with tears. As he and Tilley awkwardly made their way from the rear seat to the front door of the shack, Joe heard his satellite phone ring. Picking it up off the floor beside Verity's seat, his eyeballs hardened as if focussing on a new event amidst the chaos.

"Yes." It was more a statement than a question. "Rylan, where are you now?" Verity turned toward Joe, listening intently.

"Don't worry, Verity's safe here with me right now in the truck.

Just hold tight. I'm turning the truck around, and I'll pick up you and Buzz at the side door of The Sandpiper in fifteen minutes."

"Verity, why don't you wait here in the shack? We'll pick you up on the way back."

Verity wouldn't hear of it. "No, Joe, thanks, but it's out of the question. I couldn't bear it if anything happened to Rylan and I wasn't there when I could have been."

Joe didn't waste time arguing and set about repeating the dangerous drive back to the hotel, dodging flying objects and swerving around debris on the road. When they reached the hotel, Rylan and Buzz were already watching from the breezeway. Their struggle against the forces to fit themselves into the back section of the cab was minimal compared with what they'd already endured.

Rylan reached forward to grasp Verity's hand, bringing it up toward his lips. "Love, if anything had happened to you, I..." She'd never forget that moment, his words, and the look in his eyes.

Right there, Verity realized for the first time just how much she meant to Rylan. Even though the hurricane raged all around them, in that precious moment, they were in their own world. Verity felt her stomach thrill as she embraced the impact of Rylan's authenticity.

"Rylan, you and Buzz risked your lives for me." She cranked her body around to look Buzz in the eye and squeeze his forearm with her hand. Feeling her eyes fill with tears of gratitude, she turned to face forward again.

As she continued to express her gratitude, "I couldn't even begin to ...," the thunderous thud of a large tree limb smashing down on the box of the truck shook everyone to the core.

The sharp bark of Joe's terrier Sammy pierced the air. His trembling body and scared-stiff eyes caused Buzz to snuggle him in close, saying, "It's okay, Sammy; we're gonna come out of this okay."

Joe managed to drive away from the fallen limb, leaving it to crash to the ground. "Where're we headed, Joe?" Rylan asked from the back seat.

"As far inland as I can get," explained Joe, as the truck's tires rattled over damaged roadways and past hundreds of roofless houses, flattened structures, fences uprooted and torn apart, upended and broken trees, flooded fields, blown-out vehicles, and downed powerlines.

A brick-coloured eight-wheeled trailer with the name "DUKE" written in white capital letters on the side had been dented almost in half, putting an end to its life of service.

"Anyone know what category we're lookin' at?" asked Buzz from the back.

"Last I heard it was a four, now upgraded to five," said Joe.

"It went from category two to category five overnight," said Verity. Coming from her mouth, the words sounded foreign.

"People fled to the airport, hoping to get out before the eye of the storm hit," said Joe. "But planes weren't flying after it became too risky. And they refused to take pets, so apparently, a woman was sitting at the flooded airport with a piece of glass in her foot, holding her dog in her lap."

Verity gasped. "Oh, no, and her foot. She couldn't get medical attention, I'm sure, with the roads washed out. I sure hope it didn't get infected."

"I hope not, but that woman had it better than most. My friend Cal told me people were clinging to trees, climbing up as high as they could against the rising water level. Sometimes to no avail. There was widespread panic," he continued, "with no one being able to help anyone else."

The passengers listened attentively, beyond grateful that they'd narrowly escaped the worst part of the hurricane. "People were trapped in their houses, in their cars, without food or water. Cal saw a woman walking waist-deep in water, a backpack on her back, holding a dog in her arms."

Judith left a trail of heartbreak, tearing loved ones apart, sometimes forever, as survivors struggled in disbelief and horror at the natural disaster from which some would never recover.

"I sure hope Jacks made it safely back to Nassau," Verity said.

From the back seat, Buzz sounded concerned, "Jacks? Do you mean the Jacks who has a property near Casuarina House?"

Verity turned in her seat to look at Buzz, glancing up at Rylan, who was listening closely. The creases on Buzz's forehead deepened, and he glanced down at the floor. When he spoke, his voice was unsteady. "I, uh, no, I'm real sorry to tell you that Jacks' plane went down near Norman's Cay. It disappeared off the radar; she wouldn't've survived."

The news hit the pit of Verity's stomach like a sledgehammer. She covered her mouth with her hand, stifling her urge to scream into the closed compartment of the truck cab. Her mind raced over images of her and Jacks together on Jacks' property, in the party boat where they first met, on their weekend on Paradise Island, and the last time she saw Jacks in her plane. Tears streamed down Verity's cheeks, and she wiped them away with her hand.

Both Verity and Rylan were quiet. "Someone you knew?" asked Joe, keeping his eyes on the flooded road ahead.

"Yeah," answered Verity, her voice revealing a deep sadness over the loss of her friend. "In fact, she flew me to Abacos before heading to Nassau. That was on Monday."

"Flights weren't cancelled until Wednesday, so she must've been in the air around that time too," said Rylan.

"She could've been heading to south Florida when the storm hit. That's the usual route for drug runners in this area," said Buzz. No one replied.

Eventually, Verity turned around to look at Rylan again, whispering, "Rylan, she was delayed because of me." Tears flowed down her cheeks and she wiped them with her hands.

Rylan reached forward and squeezed Verity's shoulder. "Don't blame yourself, sweetheart. A pilot keeps abreast of weather conditions. She knew what she was doing, and it was her choice." Verity's body shook with emotion.

"Storms are unpredictable," Buzz interjected. "Here in the

Bahamas, we've lived through many hurricanes. But this one was a brute that surprised us all."

Verity turned toward Rylan, speaking softly. "At least now she won't have to face an investigation." Rylan nodded knowingly as Verity's mind flipped to a horrible thought. *I was the one who reported the break-in at Jacks' house, sparking an investigation. So, if she was afraid of going to jail and exposing her family's history in the drug trade, then she might have chosen to end her life.* Verity turned pale at the thought that she might have had anything to do with Jacks' death.

It was as if Rylan knew what she was thinking. He gathered Sammy into his arms and placed the dog on Verity's lap. "You did nothing wrong, sweetness. Don't blame yourself for anything. Truly. Choices were made a long time ago that had nothing to do with you. All you did was what any other good citizen would have done."

Verity hugged Sammy close and, turning to Rylan again, said in the cab for all to hear, "Rylan, I didn't think I could love you any more."

CHAPTER 24

Saturday, August 17 – Sunday, August 18

Hurricane Judith dissipated as swiftly as it had arrived. On Saturday afternoon, Rylan and Verity returned to Exuma, leaving Buzz to salvage his trawler. Over protests from Rylan, he insisted on doing the work himself, knowing that Rylan's time with Verity was now quite limited.

Casuarina House looked especially inviting as Verity clung to Rylan's waist, pressing against him as his motorcycle rumbled down the gravel driveway. Back home, safe in the colourful cottage, they were grateful for all their blessings, both small and large, their relationship strengthened even more by the ordeal in Abacos.

On the evening of August 17, they sat on the verandah, the warm air enveloping them, as they continued discussing the hurricane. With only one more full day before she would return to Vancouver, Verity treasured every moment more than ever before.

Protected against midges, they sipped their glasses of white wine, trying to debrief the horror of Hurricane Judith.

"Verity remarked, 'The things lost or damaged in the hurricane— they don't matter. They're replaceable. But loved ones aren't."

In the aftermath of Judith, the entire power grid of Abacos had been destroyed. There were stories of eighteen families huddled together in one shack with the water pushing in. "Only a miracle could have saved them as they were swept out to sea," said Verity, hanging her head in sorrow. After a minute, she continued, "Judith did not discriminate; no one was immune from the devastation, not women, not children, not pets. It makes you realize how fragile life is, right?"

"Rylan nodded. 'Yeah, I heard sixty-three people died, and 235 are still missing. All the shacks around Marsh Harbor were washed away, and the hotel was barely left standing."

Verity shuddered. "I can't imagine where I'd be now if you, Buzz, and Joe hadn't saved me.'" Even after having gone through it, the ordeal still seemed surreal to Verity in many ways.

They sat in silence for a while, as though needing a break from the drama. Rylan eventually took Verity by the hand as they stretched their legs and looked up at the crescent moon and the multitude of stars twinkling in the night sky.

After a minute, Rylan turned to Verity and tenderly said, "Ver, maybe you know now that you're my everything."

Verity choked inwardly when she heard pretty much the same phrase that Rick had written in his letter. *You're everything to me.*

Trying to hide her rising uneasiness, Verity buried her face in Rylan's chest. "Yeah, I read in the paper that waves surged as high as thirty feet; the water level rose as high as the third floor, and that's where my room was. It was too dangerous to carry out any rescue missions. Everyone was helpless as people and structures were swept out to sea." She knew she was babbling, trying to avoid responding more appropriately to Rylan's expression of love.

But, true to form, Rylan provided a buffer to help ease Verity back to life as it was before the hurricane.

Verity felt the vibration of Rylan's voice as she stayed resting her head against his firm chest. "And they said the wind peaked at 185 mph," Rylan noted. "I think that's about the time Buzz and I tried hanging on to the trawler railing," Rylan joked, trying to lighten the conversation.

The mood was sullen that night. Verity and Rylan felt blessed to be safe in each other's arms. "It could have been either or both of us who got swept away, Rylan." Closing her eyes as if to shut out the horror of the ordeal, Verity added, "I just couldn't bear it had you and Buzz died during your mission to save me." Her eyes welled up as she fought back the tears, and she felt that Rylan knew she needed more time to process what had happened. It wasn't that long, after all, that she'd survived a shark attack.

"I know, sweetness," Rylan replied. 'The thought of losing you drove me to act." Knowing that you were completely inexperienced in hurricane survival, I couldn't sit by and let things happen. And Buzz, well, I knew I could count on him; he's always been that way. I owe him, big-time."

"I owe both of you big-time," Verity acknowledged. "But some things can't be re-paid if you know what I mean. It's not likely that I'd be in a position of trying to save both of your lives, ha. At least, I hope not." The left side of Verity's lips curved upward slightly in sort of a half grin—a cross between a smile and a simple recognition.

Verity turned to face Rylan. She took both of his hands in hers. "There's one thing I now know for sure, babe."

Rylan's eyes widened as he waited in anticipation of Verity's words. The only sound was the gentle lapping of waves as they reached the shore. The scent of roses was heightened in the evening, a memory that Verity would carry with her in the coming months.

"There's no doubt in my mind now that you love me."

Rylan nodded, a gentle smile appearing on his lips. "So, this is what it takes to prove my love to you." They laughed together, and Verity released his hands.

"No, of course not. But in a way, I needed proof, whether that was right or wrong. And I think you knew that."

"Uh, yeah, I guess," Rylan smirked. His voice became soft as he reached over and stroked Verity's hair. "And now you know, my love; my secret's out."

They moved to the bedroom, their embrace deepening with renewed passion. Rylan placed his hand under Verity's chin, raising it to kiss her lips with such tenderness that she was transformed into jelly. Verity sighed against his mouth as he lowered her onto the bed. His warm body relaxed into hers as she dissolved into the mattress.

"I don't want us to be apart ever again," whispered Rylan. "But I know you have to leave on Monday; I get that."

"Let's not dwell on that now, love," Verity murmured." They both disappeared into that place that neither of them ever wanted to forget—their 'Forever Place,' a sanctuary they both cherished.

IN THE GENTLE light of Sunday morning, Rylan asked, "Will you be coming back to me?"

"I'll happily answer your question once we get up, get dressed, and move out to our breakfast corner on the verandah? I'll make some French toast if you like."

"I like," Rylan agreed, smiling, "but only if you have some of that real Canadian maple syrup you brought with you." He raised his brows in playful anticipation. "And I'll put on the coffee."

After breakfast, they lingered over a second cup of coffee when Verity leaned over and kissed Rylan's cheek.

"You're making me nervous, sweetness," he said, his knee bouncing slightly.

"Oh, no, please don't be. What I want to say is that there are few things I know for sure in this life. But one of them is that you love me, and I love you. Period."

"Aw, you love me too, babe?" Rylan teased, his dimples deepening with joy.

"With all my heart, Rylan."

"Then why not just stay here?" He reached over, placing his hand on her thigh.

"Because I have a few things to take care of back home. All my belongings are in my apartment rental. I can't just abandon everything."

"Well, actually, you could."

"C'mon, babe; quit teasing. There's a way to do things, and being irresponsible isn't my way."

"Ha, then perhaps I've seen a side of you that you didn't show while living here in Exuma," he laughed, then decided to rein in that line of thought.

"I think you're probably right on that issue," Verity laughed.

"Okay," Rylan said, turning serious. "And are you planning on seeing Rick while you're there?"

"Yes," Verity paused, gauging his reaction. His face remained expressionless.

Before Verity could continue, Rylan rose from his chair and stretched, linking his fingers above his head. At that moment, they both noticed two figures walking hand-in-hand on the beach, one of whom was the platinum-haired Gina.

"Ah, looks like Gina's still with Luca."

"Luca?" Verity asked, "Who's that?"

"Her new man friend. He's the talk of Georgetown and beyond. A charming Italian who owns a property on Emerald Bay."

"A druggie?" Verity inquired, suspecting she already knew the answer.

"Rumor has it that the guy's clean. And the most intriguing part is that Gina is supposedly trying to clean up her act too."

"Oh, that *is* intriguing, Rylan. I guess you'll miss her attention," Verity teased.

Rylan smirked. "Let's just hope the relationship lasts. That'd be good not only for my well-being but for yours."

Verity laughed. "Yeah, not having to be on high alert every time

I'm with that woman would be a nice change. And did you know that Gina encouraged me to go to Abacos?"

Rylan's eyes widened as he turned to her.

"Yes, she knew that Jacks had agreed to fly me there on Monday, and, as you know, all flights were cancelled by Wednesday. I mean, she must have known about the hurricane warnings, don't you think?"

"Ha, everyone knew, babe; you'd have to live under a, uh, sorry. I know you don't listen to the news and, unless someone told you, how could you have known?"

"My neglect, no argument there. But, if you could have seen how exuberant Gina was; she was almost insistent that I go."

Gina interrupted their conversation as she walked down the white stone steps toward the verandah. Luca waited by the beach.

"Verity," she called, "can we talk for a moment, please?" She smiled briefly at Rylan, who did not return the sentiment.

Verity glanced at Rylan and murmured, "What does she want now?" implying there was always an agenda with Gina.

Verity approached Gina, who had stepped to the side of the property, out of Rylan's earshot.

"Ver," Gina began, "I want to apologize sincerely." She hung her head as though in shame.

Verity wanted to hear the words directly. "For?"

Gina cleared her throat and met Verity's gaze. "Oh, honey, for encouraging you to go to Abacos when I knew a hurricane was building. And it was obvious you hadn't heard. I suspect you have no experience dealing with a hurricane."

"Well, you got that right, Gina. But tell me, why would you do such a thing? Do you hate me so much that you'd be happy to see me in harm's way? I assume you know that lives were lost, and there was immeasurable suffering. Was that your wish for me, Gina?" Verity's eyes welled up with tears.

"No, no," Gina said, "the truth is I like you very much, Verity."

She hung her head again and said in a lower voice, "I just didn't want to see you with Rylan, and that's the truth. That's the whole ugly truth of it."

Even though Verity heard her clearly, she pretended she did not. "Say that again, Gina. You just didn't want to...what?"

CHAPTER 25

*T*uesday, August 1

As Verity's plane ascended from the Georgetown airport, her thoughts drifted to the memories she cherished with Rylan. She recalled the vibrant flame tree he had planted in his garden—a symbol of their enduring love. Its fiery red blossoms, reminiscent of the arrival of spring, mirrored the intensity and passion of their relationship.

Rylan had introduced her to a world filled with lightness, laughter, passion, and unwavering care. In his presence, she felt a profound connection, as if no one else mattered. He became her sanctuary, her release from the world's burdens, and her one true love.

Eager to embrace their shared future, Verity anticipated returning to Exuma. She knew she needed to meet with Rick to gently convey her decision, but her heart belonged to Rylan. Their bond was unbreakable, and she was ready to build a life with him, surrounded by the beauty and serenity of Exuma.

THE VERITY CHILD TRILOGY

Don't miss the other books in the Verity Child Women's Fiction Trilogy. From workplace chaos in the Big City to finding love on the dreamy island of Exuma, this captivating trilogy offers a vivid, emotional journey.

In the prequel, Nicole leaves behind her stifling small-town life in Ontario, hoping to discover her true self. But is she chasing her dreams—or heading for disaster?

In *The Troublemakers*, Verity pours her heart and soul into doing what's right. As a young woman with an unwavering sense of justice, she risks everything—even her career—to stand by her principles. Will her determination be enough, or will doing the right thing come at too great a cost?

ABOUT THE AUTHOR

<u>Maren Hill</u>

Captivated by the intrigue of everyday life, Maren Hill writes heart-felt, emotional stories that celebrate women and the relationships that shape their lives.

Quirky, good-hearted characters you'd love to know, and stories laced with romance, humour, compassion, and inspiration are trade-marks of Maren Hill's books.

<u>J.D. Monk</u>

Written by children's book author JD Monk, *Slimy Slick* appeals to both children and adults with fascinating facts about banana slugs.

If you enjoy my books, <u>please leave a review.</u> There's nothing more motivational than positive reviews. Thank you so much.

ALSO BY MAREN HILL

Cliffhouse Footprints

Cliffhouse by the Sea

Sunrise Island Sisters

Sunrise Island Christmas

Sunrise Island Celebrations

Nicole
The Troublemakers
Our Forever Place

Make a Spectacular Seashell Lamp
Sealed with a Kiss

WHAT READERS SAY

"Maren Hill's description of the island is so real that you can smell the salt air, feel the sand between your toes, the sun sparkling on the water, and hear the waves. Maren Hill weaves her stories extremely well."

"... she has a real knack for transporting the reader to the world of the story."

"The characters are great and the story is ... captivating."

"Awesome. Great setting, and relatable characters with solid backgrounds. Well written... character portrayal is solid with depth."

"... a suspenseful and mysterious story... will keep you on the edge of your seat."

"Excellent knack for transporting the reader into the world of the story... I can't wait for more. A true gem!"

"I thoroughly enjoyed ... Cliffhouse by the Sea... kept me wanting to know what would happen next."

"Maren Hill has done it again! Love this book. Would definitely read more by her."

"This story with Alexa and Kyla was riveting. I really enjoyed the dynamics of these two sisters. This is a great story."

"Beautifully done and exceptionally entertaining, heart-wrenching and delightful.

"Gorgeous writing! I love the author's rich descriptions of characters, scenes and situations - I felt like I was living it."

"JD Monk writes with a simplicity that pulls kids into the story immediately, but also with an underlying complexity and intelligence that allows the ideas in Slimy Slick to stay with them long after the tale ends. Well done!"

"This is a great story. Congratulations to the author for bringing awareness to these little creatures who are often misunderstood and undervalued. I love the education/entertainment combo. The illustrations are engaging and hilarious."

"Beautifully written and illustrated -- this is a wonderful bedtime story! Not only do we learn about the importance of banana slugs in our ecosystem in this story, but we're introduced to lovely language to increase the richness of our vocabulary. This is an awesome gift for children (and their parents) who are curious about their environment!"

"What a wonderful read! It was extremely informative about Banana Slugs; a very misunderstood creature. I learned a lot! The graphics are very well done! Definitely a must buy this Holiday Season for the little ones in the family!"

"Loved this book! Very well written, easy to understand and follow for children! Super informative as well, I had no idea slugs were this unique!"

"I have a whole new appreciation for slugs...The kids love it."

"... full of amazing facts about slugs... Completely recommend for curious kids who love nature."

"The fun facts were marvelous and very informative. 5 stars to the author. Highly recommend."

"Great book, full of lots of interesting slug facts. I recommend this for all young and young-at-heart bug lovers."

"Perfect for storytime and a wonderful way to explore nature!"

SLIMY SLICK—NOT JUST FOR KIDS!

The Nighttime Adventures of a Banana Slug

This captivating picture book appeals to kids and adults through multiple reads and is jam-packed with suspense, slime, and fun facts.

Join Slimy Slick on his exciting nighttime adventure through the countryside as he glides toward the tasty treat of his dreams. He encounters an earthworm and a shrew, but the real danger lies ahead. Will Slick's journey come to an abrupt end at the hands of a well-meaning boy whose mission is to capture and eliminate? Does he not understand Slick's important role in the ecosystem?

Readers learn about the clever design of the banana slug and how Slick uses his natural gifts to protect himself and navigate life in the wild.

Discover the world of Slimy Slick through a rainforest adventure that educates and entertains, emphasizing the importance of these fascinating creatures to our planet.

Perfect for:

• Parents and grandparents, science teachers, librarians, educators

• Gifts for kids who love nature, rainforest animals, and learning more about the natural world and zoology

• Read-aloud family sharing

• Gaining environmental wisdom

• Understanding empathy and collaboration

ACKNOWLEDGMENTS

To every woman who has ever taken a chance on something as beautifully unpredictable as love. May we all find the love we seek. And may we recognize it when it finally arrives.